# Entwined

## Book 3 of A New Life Series

### Samantha Jacobey

# Entwined

## Book 3 of A New Life Series

## Samantha Jacobey

## Lavish Publishing, LLC ~ Houston

First Edition
2015 Lavish Publishing, LLC
Book 3 of A New Life Series
All Rights Reserved
Published in the United States by Lavish Publishing, LLC, Houston
Cover Design by: Nicolene Lorette Design
Cover Images: SHUTTERSTOCK
Paperback ISBN
ISBN: **0615996493**
ISBN-13: **978-0615996493**
www.LavishPublishing.com

# Table of Contents

# Prologue

Glancing down at the number of the incoming call, Michael Anderson flipped open his phone, "Yeah."

"Hey, Mike, how you doin' little brother?" drawled a familiar male voice.

"Hey Henry, I'm good I guess. Long time no hear," his tone jovial, he sounded pleased to get word from his older sibling.

"Oh, ya know, life on the road. Listen, I gotta make this quick. Eddie's got a job that needs doin'. Was hopin' to put ya up for it."

"Eddie Farrell? Ah, you know I just got out a few months ago. Been thinking about finding a different way of life. Figure I got enough blood on my hands." Having worked with the group a couple of times in the past, Michael knew what his brother's crew, the Dragons, were into and had hoped to stay clear of it.

"Naw, man," Henry turned on the charm, "It's not a hit. Real easy job. Long term, too. He's got some guy he needs looked after. No blood and guts. Easy money."

Michael rocked his jaw side to side as he deliberated the offer. "Where you wanna meet?" he finally relented; *might as well, right?*

Henry released a quiet laugh. He knew his baby brother wouldn't say no. He gave him an address to a small bar in Little Rock, "Two days from now, 'bout eightish, meet ya in the back."

Michael stared at the phone for a moment before returning it to his pocket, a dull ache in the pit of his stomach. *I always do what my big brother wants;* he sighed. *Someday, I'm gonna learn to make my own way. Just not today.*

# Indelible

Peeking out through the swinging doors that led onto the sales floor, Michael could see his target standing inside the counter to his right, watching the contestants keenly. Allowing the door to close, he nervously walked away, knowing he would soon make his move.

He had noticed the girl a few days ago, when they had been in and out of the shop for the autograph session. Ever since then, he had been waiting, not so patiently, for the right time to make his presence known. *This's it,* he reassured himself. *Time for me to keep my word.* He knew he could ignore his promise, but then he would be letting his brother down. *Can't have that.*

Shuffling in a large circle, he continued to pace the floor. Stopping next to the work bench, he ran his fingers through his thick brown hair, his mind going over exactly what he would say for the umpteenth time.

It had been over four years since they last met, and he wasn't sure how she would take his suddenly showing up there, without any warning. His mouth dry, he licked at his lips anxiously. *God, I can't take this,* he thought to himself with a shake of his head. *I don't even like this girl. But Henry does...*

Once again at the double doors, he could see her making her way up to the stage, carrying a white guitar. Moving out into the crowd, he took a position next to the glass counter on the right. He panned the crowd; *this is a pretty tame group, considering*. Watching as she made it to the front, he leaned his rear end against the glass, tapping his boot anxiously.

Tori spoke into the mic, "Hey, Collin honey, this is for you," nodding in his direction.

Michael grinned at his employer's surprised expression, as he sat only a few feet from him at the moment. *Nice... this'll be good.* He had seen the girl in action back in the day. *Yeah, she's hot, if you like it nasty. I'm sure they had a real good time.*

Strumming the guitar, she began to sing. Her voice strong as she belted out the lines of her song, the first verse seemed to be about her past. Michael surveyed the crowd again, only half listening while watching for signs of trouble.

His mind shifted easily over the four days he spent with the Dragons; he recalled the group with a smirk. *I know exactly who and what she is... the kind of girl who enjoys spreading it around.* He folded his arms across his chest as he looked back towards the raised platform; *Nobody's Angel my ass.*

Hitting the second verse, she sang about not letting the booze touch her lips nor lying with men, because she was still Nobody's Angel. Michael chuckled. From what he had seen, he couldn't imagine a girl like that ever telling a man no. *Whatever you say, baby girl. Old habits die hard.*

Listening to the final verse, he felt his palms go sweaty, as she professed to be a murderer. "*I'm a cold hearted bitch... that'll put you in the ground... And when I die, I'll do my time in hell... because after all, I am... Nobody's Angel.*" Her voice held deep emotion as her hands moved through the riffs.

Michael's blood ran cold. *Was that a threat?* Standing up straight, he could hear his pulse in his ears, pounding like a hammer, his eyes darting between Collin and the front of the crowd. *What the hell was that shit?* The Dragons were a horrific group of hired thugs, and she had been their whore; a typical needy woman from what he had seen. *Riding with them don't make you a badass, sweetheart.*

He could tell there had been some commotion going on with the judges while she played, but he hadn't bothered to move any closer to investigate. Peering through the large number of people before him, he could see the head judge taking over the mic, announcing she wasn't really a contestant.

Struggling to focus, he heard her quip, "Pfft, I already won," as she scoffed at the official, "I got the chance to play." She practically leapt off the platform and headed his way. Stopping to grab her jacket from the end of the glass, she shoved on the doors and headed into the back, not giving him a second glance.

Quickly, Michael turned on his heel and followed her, noting she seemed too lost in her own thoughts and adrenaline to be aware of him. He could hear the audience cheering, and he puffed into his cupped palms to calm himself. *No need to be nervous, just stick to the plan.* Tori made it to the office door and stopped abruptly, still carrying the guitar.

Michael whipped around her, taking a position between her and the smaller entrance. *Wow, she's beautiful… not like the picture.* His mind flashed the image frozen on a photo he carried in his wallet; the one Eddie had sent him.

Tori had been grinning like a fool when their eyes met, but it quickly fell away. Michael's mind halted, and a single word fell from his lips, "Hi." For an instant, she stood staring at him, then shoved the guitar into his chest and turned her back on him.

Thinking quickly, he followed while calling her name, but she ploughed into the crowd, and he could see her disappear out through the exit before he could get even close to catching her. *Damn it.* Looking around wildly, he caught sight of the kid who had told him about the scar on her face, confirming her identity.

Pushing through the throng of people, he handed the boy the guitar and shouted over the noise, "Hey! Where's she going?" indicating the exit.

Surprised, Max gave a shrug, not even realizing Tori had left the building. Together, they weaved their way over to the single glass door and outside, coming face to face with Terral Huffman.

Terry stood toe to toe with him, staring him straight in the eye. "What the hell do you think you're doing?" he demanded, edging towards him in a slow challenge.

Taken off guard, Michael moved back, considering how to explain the situation to the shop owner. "Hey, I'm just checkin' on the girl," he stammered. With a shake of his head and a raised hand, he indicated the figure that had rapidly scurried away, "I think I scared her when she came in the back. Sorry, that wasn't my intention."

Terry knew this man came in with the band, head of their personal security team, in fact, and had met him several times over the last few weeks. He also knew he had held the position for years. Staring into the man's eyes, Terry replayed Tori's words, "*I have to leave, right now. There's a man from my past in the back, which means trouble.*" She had been terrified, and he had let her go, returning to buy time for her to get away.

Realizing who the man was, he felt somewhat confused. "You better do some fast talking," Terry's tone remained menacing as he glared at him, holding his ground.

Michael drew a deep breath, no longer able to see the young woman as he squinted down the sidewalk. *Fuck me, she's gone!*

Looking back at Terry, he nodded his agreement, "But not here. We should go inside, to the office, where we can talk in private." With him leading the way, Terry followed, telling Max to get the customers taken care of as quickly as possible, so the store could be closed on time.

Pushing their way back through the crowd and clearing the swinging doors, Terry noted the band members also in the back. He could only assume they were taking refuge from the chaos out front. He didn't wait for any explanations and began in a booming voice, "Ok, what the hell is going on here?" Obviously pissed, no one in his right mind would want to cross him.

Brian and Collin shared a quick glance at one another, and then hung their heads, avoiding the older man's stare. They held guilty expressions, knowing they had not been fair to the young woman who had been on the stage a few minutes before. However, neither of them wanted in on the conversation, and were tempted to face the mob on the sales floor rather than hang around in the midst of what looked to be a tirade in the making.

"Alright, alright, alright" Michael adjusted his stance, trying to wave the accusations off with his hands. "I know her. Knew her." He shifted his eyes to his employers, acutely aware things could get ugly if he said too much. "My brother rode with the group who raised her." Having made his choice, he realized the path would be tricky to navigate.

"About a year ago, my brother contacted me. Said he was gonna send her to me so I could look out for her," Michael calmly explained, "But she never showed up, and I haven't heard from him since."

Terry drew in a deep breath, his voice a little less irritated, "So who's your brother?" *Tori murdered the Dragons seven months ago... either this guy don't know that, or maybe he's looking for revenge.*

"Henry Morgan," Michael answered directly. "He was pretty much an outcast in the group since he didn't like the way the Dragons treated her. He had been forbidden to touch her or speak to her for years. Now, I really need to talk to her. Could you *please* tell me where I can find her?"

Hearing the hint of desperation in his voice, Terry nodded slowly, "I know where she's staying." He knew Henry had been someone Tori had trusted. Giving him another up and down inspection, he felt unsure if he completely believed Michael's motives.

In the back of his mind, curiosity tickled him, *why run from Henry's brother?* However, he knew there had been a great deal of her story he wasn't privy to and hated to second guess her where the men from her past were concerned. *Besides, it don't sound like he knows his brother's dead, and I'm not gonna be the one to tell him.*

Suspecting the dispute had nothing to do with their behavior, Collin and Brian gained a bit of confidence, and demanded to be told what they were getting at.

Michael turned to face the two men squarely, considering the need to cut them loose and get on with finding the girl. He had applied for the job as their personal head of security under Eddie's say so. Therefore, it had only been a means to an end, and he had no real qualms about giving it up.

On the other hand, his brother had given him a more important job – looking after Tori Farrell. *Henry loves that girl*, Michael recalled, and he would see to it she was safe for him, no matter the cost. *Besides, she can tell me where Henry is,* and that made him even more eager to talk to her.

Out of respect, he tried to be diplomatic. "Sorry guys, I'm afraid I need to resign, effective immediately. This girl's really important to me. It was a great gig, and I think I did a pretty decent job at it, but it's time for goodbye." Turning back to Terry, he pushed on, "Just give me the address, and I can find my own way. I need to get moving though, before she gets too far ahead of me." He tossed a thumb over his shoulder to indicate the need for urgency.

Terry shifted his weight from one foot to the other, considering his options. "Just a sec," he raised a hand and went into the office to stall him.

Closing the door for privacy, he called the halfway house and Brandon answered on the first ring. "Yeah, Brandon, this's Terry. I need to talk to Tori, ASAP."

He listened semi-patiently while Brandon informed him that she had already been and gone. Comparing notes, the house manager filled him in as to the events from the second location, and discussed how Tori had not wanted to wait around for any explanations or further surprises.

"You're certain she's gone?" Terry asked in a stern voice.

"Yeah," Brandon confirmed, "Sharon just walked in from dropping her at the bus station. She's definitely gone. Besides, are you sure you can trust that guy? Tori's a pretty smart girl... if she ran from him, there had to be a reason."

"Yeah, that's what bothers me," Terry nodded into the device. "Got a lot of unanswered questions. Thanks though." He laid the phone in its cradle. Sitting back to think for a moment, he blinked rapidly as if trying to focus, deciding what to do next. Hearing the sound of raised voices, he got to his feet and moved to investigate.

Opening the door, he exited the office to discover a small argument had erupted between Michael and the band members. Michael's voice had become raised as he defended himself, "Look, it don't matter. All I can tell you is, I gotta go; it's my job to take care of her. How and why are *my* business. I'm glad you guys think so highly of me you want me to stay, but this isn't my priority. If I lose her now, I might never find her again. Just get somebody else. Really guys, it's not *that* big of a deal." Shifting his gaze as Terry rejoined the group, "Well?" he impatiently demanded.

For a moment, Tori's friend considered Michael's words and actions, and the fact he had been security with the band for so long. The older man knew, in the end it would be his call. Finally making his selection, he drew a deep breath and exhaled slowly, "She's already gone. They dropped her at the bus station, and no one knows which way she's headed."

Michael's face lit up immediately; *that's all I need,* folding his hands in front of his face as if he were praying, "Thank you," he clamored. "Sorry guys, but I gotta go catch her or find out where she's goin'." Turning abruptly, he made for the exit.

For a moment, Terry deliberated letting him leave, then trotted after him, "Hang on and I'll give you a ride." Leaving Derrick in charge with instructions to get the customers handled and out of the store as soon as the finalists had been announced, the pair made their way out to Terry's car that awaited them down the street.

# One Way Ride

Sitting in the front seat of Terry's vehicle, Michael stared out of the window, nervously clinching his fists to try and calm himself. "She didn't give you any idea where she's headed?"

Deep in thought, Terry shook his head, but said nothing.

"Jesus," Michael, leaned on his elbow and chewed his finger. "I don't know enough to find her if she's already gone. I mean, it's been over four years since I even saw her last, back before I took the job with the band. I have no idea who she knows or where she would go." He ran his fingers through his short curls again, obviously disturbed. *Damn it. No word in a fucking year, then poof, there she is; I've gotta find her and get to the bottom of this.*

Terry exhaled loudly, "Relax. I can find out where she went. But I want you to promise me one thing."

Michael looked over at him, waiting to hear his demands.

"You promise me you're really gonna take care of her. And you make sure you contact me if anything ever happens or you need anything." He reached into the ash tray and handed him a business card to the store.

Michael stared down at the smooth finish, considering if he might be one of her numerous lovers, and then nodded generously, "You've got my word on that." He placed the card into his wallet behind his ID; *I already promised Henry to look out for her, what would another one hurt?*

17

Pulling up at the station, the pair went inside and approached the woman behind the counter. Michael stood out of the way while Terry spoke to the attendant, who seemed reluctant to help. After a few minutes, the shop owner walked away, a slip of paper in his hand.

Back outside the front doors, he explained, "Ok, she's still here. Her bus leaves in an hour, so you've got that long to locate her." He handed Michael the sheet of paper with the word Denver written on it, the time 9:55 pm, and *one way ticket* scrawled underneath.

Michael stared down at it for a moment, and then shook the extended hand enthusiastically. "Don't worry," he reassured the older man, "I won't let anything happen to her."

Terry nodded and walked away, headed back to his car at a quick gait.

Michael glanced around the station for a moment, assessing where he should start his search. Then, thinking better of it, he strolled up to the window and handed the girl the paper, "Are there any seats left on this bus?"

She looked at him with a confused expression, then pulled up the screen to sell him a spot. "You want next to the girl?" she asked absently.

"Yeah, sure, that'd be great, thanks," he responded, *actually that would be perfect.*

Ticket in hand, Michael exited through the glass door to the front instead of into the waiting area. He had decided to stick to the shadows and board the bus at the last minute. If she were there, he would sit down, and they would be leaving together. If not, he would get off the bus and decide what to do next. Finding a stone bench outside the entry to the station, he wanted to avoid her seeing him until she became captive to the moving transport.

Sitting in the early darkness, the air warm around him, he

reached into his back pocket to pull out his wallet and remove the only picture he kept there. Staring down at the image, his thumb slid lightly across the glossy finish. He thought about how stunning she had looked a short while ago, the same as she had the first time he had seen her four years ago. *Henry's girl,* his mind recalled absently.

Michael wasn't really a sentimental kind of guy. He didn't hold onto mementos, such as photographs, and his list of personal belongings had always been sparse. However, this particular picture vexed him, mostly because of the man who had taken it: Eddie Farrell.

The Farrell boys were evil men, maybe the darkest he had ever met. At odd times, he would pull out the old Polaroid and ponder the girl, his brother, and the confusing world in which they lived, glad he had avoided joining it.

Replacing the picture and returning his wallet to its place, he began to watch the giant clock on the outside of the station. At ten minutes to departure, he made his way to the loading area. Not having any baggage, he easily made it out and into the line quickly.

Examining the side of the bus while he followed the line around to the door, he saw the shape of someone leaning against the glass, left arm covering their face. At the sight of the black leather jacket, his heart began to pound in anticipation, pretty sure he had located his target.

The time ticked down, and his plan worked perfectly. Moments before the bus pulled out of the station, he climbed the steps to board the giant vehicle. He saw her immediately, and caught his breath as he noticed how happy she appeared, obviously thinking she had gotten away.

Swallowing hard, Michael made his way down the aisle and slowly sank into the seat beside her. Staring at her profile, he waited for her to notice him. Smiling when she looked up, her expression quickly crumbled, and he could hear the emotion in her voice when she stammered, "What're you doing here?"

His eyes flitted down to her glossy lips, then back up to her pale blue eyes. "Going to Denver," he answered flatly.

Twisting away from him, she looked out the window as they pulled out onto the road. He could tell she was upset, but he tried to remain calm. They had an eight hour ride ahead of them, and he would do his best to make her understand his intentions were benevolent within that time. After letting her cool down for a few minutes, he probed softly, "Can I ask you a question?"

The girl made no reply, and sat staring out into the darkness while biting her thumb nail. He knew she could hear him, so he continued. "How did you get away from the Dragons?" His voice calm, he waited for her reply.

She sat for a moment, her movements giving away her heightened level of tension when she turned swiftly to face him. "What's it to you?" she demanded, eyes narrowed.

Opening a palm to the roof, Michael replied coolly, "I'm curious."

Tori furiously spit her reply, "It's none of your damn business." She drew a sharp breath before she went on, lifting her chin as she challenged him, "You got all you're gonna get from me last time we saw each other. So shut up, and leave me alone." She snapped her gaze back to the glass on her left and the darkness beyond.

Rocking his jaw from side to side for a moment, Michael considered her words carefully as he studied her silhouette in the dim light. *Wow,* he thought to himself; *she thinks I fucked her.* Adjusting himself in his seat, he wasn't sure how to handle the situation. His mind racing, he slowly drifted back to the few days he had spent in the company of the Dragons, and how things had all come about.

# Tainted Trophy

Michael had only been out of the army a few months when he received the call from his brother. He had always followed in his older brother's footsteps, kind of taking his lead. So when Henry called to say he had a job for him, well, he wasn't eager to work for the Dragons, but he wasn't going to turn it down either.

He met up with the group in Little Rock and rode with them a total of four days. He had a vague idea of what he was walking into, but he figured he could handle it; get the job and get on with a new way of life.

When he arrived, Henry Morgan had greeted him with a hearty handshake and made sure he knew the crew. That is, he presented him to all of the men of the group. They also had a girl with them, young and beautiful, but sullen, that Henry pretended didn't exist.

Michael had tried to be polite, and she had snubbed him, obviously not interested in making his acquaintance. He had assumed there was some kind of bad blood between her and Henry, which carried over to him on principle. Didn't really matter much, as far as he figured; he knew the Dragon's take on women… only good for one thing, and disposable at that, so she wouldn't be around for long.

The first night, he watched in amazement as darkness fell. The meek young woman who hadn't spoken hardly a word to anyone stripped off her clothes and became the life

21

of the party. She made the rounds easy enough, fucking several of the men and making quite a show of it. He had kept his distance, out of the way to watch while she worked her magic.

In the end, he had seen enough to know she was the group slut and into some very nasty sex. At the time, he had suspected that was the reason she had been with them and not dead in a ditch someplace, as they were the kind of men to enjoy her special brand of company. He deduced that she was actually part of the outfit, as much as a woman could be, and they kept her around as long as she made herself useful, which it appeared she was quite good at being useful.

For three days, Michael did his best to impress Eddie and win his favor, and thereby the job that needed doing. The afternoon of the third day, the group stopped for a late lunch at a truck stop, and he finally had a few minutes alone with his brother. He hoped he would gain some insight into how his chances were looking, and the two of them wandered away from the pack long enough to have a quick conversation.

As soon as they were in private, Henry had asked him point blank, "So whatdaya think?"

"Yeah, I can do it, if Eddie wants to give it to me. Sounds real easy, and clean, like you said." He spoke eagerly, having warmed up to the idea since he had been with the group.

"No, stupid," the older man shook his head, "About the girl."

Michael had stared at him, at a loss for several seconds. "You mean the whore? What about her? She's a nasty cunt. What'd she do, run away from home to join up with you guys? She likes to fuck; that's for sure."

Henry had given him an icy stare so cold, Michael could still feel the chill. "Naw man, we raised her," his words were barely above a whisper. "She's the real reason I asked you t' come here. I wanna get her outta all o' this." Wafting his hand around, he indicated the muck the group carried with them.

"Eddie found her some place when she was a tiny thing. We took her t' Brazil, t' that old camp we keep down there. Had her fifteen years, teachin' her… well, everything; all that we could."

"Brazil? I thought you were on vacation down there or some shit like that." The few cards and letters he had received from the area over the years flashed to mind, and no mention of training camps had ever been made, much less a girl.

Henry's brown orbs stared at his brother, boring into him. "No, it waddn't no vacation," he licked at his lips anxiously, "She knows her place. Does her job real good. If you think she does that shit 'cause she wants to, you ain' watchin' close enough." He walked away, shaking his head, leaving Michael to consider his words until they could speak again.

That evening, when dark approached, the group pulled in at a small motel. Gathering the group around, Eddie announced his decision; the job would go to Michael. To celebrate, he presented him with the girl for the night.

Immediately, Red spoke up, stipulating he still wanted his share first, but he would leave her to their fresh cohort afterwards, and Eddie agreed that would work, giving his newest crony a wink.

Michael could feel his gut wrench at the thought of touching her after what he had seen her do with the rest of the group. However, he would never let on he wasn't thrilled with the offer, *that would be an ignorant move in this crowd.* Giving Eddie a short nod, he agreed that sounded like a plan, and they shook on the deal for good measure.

Getting a few rooms, the three of them were given one to share, and Michael grew more anxious. *How am I gonna get*

23

*out of fucking the nasty bitch and catching whatever she's sharing?* He pondered his options on the way to their room, and he noticed she seemed to be flirting with Red pretty heavily as they made their way inside. *Wonder if he's her favorite? If so, I might be able to use that to somehow get out of it...*

When they entered the small chamber, Michael led the way, pausing to have a look around once inside. He heard the door shut, followed by the sound of Red punching the girl in the back, knocking her to the floor at his feet.

Immediately, he had reached down to help her, forgetting that wasn't the place to be a gentleman. When their eyes met, he could have sworn he saw real fear, but she quickly wiped it away, and it surprised him that she didn't cry; *most girls go to bawling when you're slapping them around.*

Instead, she grabbed his arm and pushed him back to sit in a large chair to watch. He noticed that she reeked of alcohol as she leaned over him, and it occurred to him she might be drunk; that could explain the lack of tears.

The girl soothed him, stroking his hair and neck with a gentle touch, and he fought the urge to push her off of him when she kissed his lips lightly. She nuzzled his cheek with her nose intimately and whispered, "Just watch, love," before Red ended their interaction, using her hair to pull her back to his side of the room.

*I ain't your love, bitch*, Michael wiped at his cheek and ran his arm across his lips where she had touched him. Folding his hands in front of his face, interlocking the digits, he used his index fingers to tap nervously on his lips. He tried to remain calm, and allow the scene to unfold before him.

He found keeping his cool difficult, as Red had a grasping hold on the girl and handled her roughly. Michael didn't like men who abused women, even ones who were willing to play along. He had seen this shit before, and quite frankly had no desire to watch the kinky sex the couple obviously enjoyed. *Ok Henry, I'm watching, and she's looking pretty into this.*

Twisting out of his grasp, the young woman began to remove her clothing, kicking off her boots and throwing them towards the dresser while unbuttoning her pants. As she pulled and lowered them, she wiggled her rear end to work them down, and Michael noticed how Red stepped back to stare, a crooked grin on his face. *Yeah, they've played this game before.*

When she tugged her shirt over her head, she pulled her hair through it and tossed it around in an exaggerated motion. Bending over, she unhooked her bra, sliding the straps down her arms and threw it onto the pile forming a few feet away. *Wonder if she acts this way when Henry fucks her. And why does he think she's faking this shit...?*

Red moved back towards her, this time standing so he could pull her body hard against his. Licking and biting at her face and neck, he slipped his hands down into her panties and began to stroke the crack of her rear end, continuing to push against her. Michael noted that she smiled and cooed as he worked her; *I think you're being played, bro.*

Red pushed her away and grasped the button on his pants, pulled them open and unzipped them with one hand. Reaching in, he grasped himself and yanked it out, stroking it roughly. He grinned at the girl, a look between eager and angry.

She immediately dropped to her knees, licking him playfully. She took the end of it into her mouth and began taking it in deeper until it slid down her throat; she worked him in and out for several minutes before pushing him back, a wide grin on her lips. *Oh yeah. She's lovin' this.*

Red left welts the shape of his right hand all over her,

which she endured in silence, actually looking pleased with his actions as she nuzzled him affectionately. *If she's pretending, she's one hell of an actress.*

While he watched, Michael's thoughts churned, and he considered what he had seen and his brother's words. *"We taught her everything." Ok, so you turned her into a whore.* Realistically, he knew nothing about the girl, not her name, her age, nothing. After hearing his brother's take on the situation, he wasn't sure how all of the pieces fit; *it don't make any sense.*

When Red had had enough, he pulled back on her hair to remove her mouth, and she grabbed the sides of his jeans to pull them down for him and help him out of them. Once freed, he released her and she stood and removed her panties before climbing onto the bed and bending over onto all fours. She stuck her rear end out and leaned on her elbows to grip the bedspread. Michael could see her knuckles go white, but her face appeared calm, almost trance like. *Oh man, now what?*

She had turned at an angle to him, so Michael wasn't able to see what Red did, but he had a pretty good idea. The other man used a small tube to grease the way with his fingers for several seconds, then pulling himself up behind her.

Michael gripped his hands tighter, realizing he really didn't want to see the action anyways, it being an act that always disgusted him and he would never take part in. *God, she's nasty; you can't tell me she's not into this...*

The girl relaxed into the motion of his body as Red bumped against her, making small grunts that punctuated the sounds of their bodies slapping together. Red used her hair to gain leverage while he fucked her, causing Michael to wince at the idea of it. Eventually, she lost her grip and slid towards the edge a bit.

Red corrected by pulling back harder on her mane for a moment; then he shoved her on forward and changed his angle of entry enough to finish the job. Michael then had a clear view of the action, and simply glared at the couple. *You guys… are disgusting.*

He noted the blood on Red's softening flesh as when withdrew. Red seemed pleased at the sight of it, laughing while he cleaned himself and got dressed, leaving the girl lying on the bed. She lay still, watching with wide eyes, as if she were waiting for something. *Yeah, like I'm gonna touch you…*

Red left them, still jovial at their antics, and closed the door loudly as he departed. Michael didn't move, and sat glaring at her, half expecting her to get up and try to put her moves on him again. *Stay down, bitch. No need to make me call you a nasty cunt to your face.*

A few minutes later, he realized she had lost consciousness. Thinking about the way she had smelled when they first entered the room, he stood quickly to run his fingers along her cheek and neck to locate her pulse. Relieved to find it, he stroked her hair out of the way as she breathed into the twisted bedding.

With a firm tug, he managed to cover her nakedness, noticing the blood and body fluids that had oozed out of her and formed a dark splotch on her inner thigh. For a moment, he thought he might to be sick. *Henry, you're a damned fool.*

Swinging his eyes around the room, he realized he could not leave. They all believed he was enjoying his prize at the moment, and snubbing the offering could hold serious consequences. He had to wait it out, even if he didn't touch her. Removing his jacket, he kicked off his boots and dropped onto the chair in disgust.

No softy, Michael had seen some bad shit, hell even done some bad shit in his time. However, he had come to realize that really wasn't the life that he wanted to live. He had hoped this would be his chance to get away from it. He wanted no part in the world the Dragons lived in. His being there didn't change that, and neither would Eddie's job.

His mind returned to his brief conversation with his older sibling earlier that day. *Get her away from them; that's what he said. But what if she don't wanna go?* Leaned back in the chair, *sorry Henry, but she looks pretty happy here,* he drifted off to sleep, his mind still working through the puzzle and moving in circles.

His sleep broken, Michael awoke a few times with a start, disturbed by his dreams. Eventually, he decided he had waited long enough to pass for the intended purpose, so he got up and slipped his boots back on. Grabbing his jacket, he closed the door quietly behind him.

The instant the cool night air hit him, he felt angry. He didn't like having to endure watching whatever the hell was going on in the shadows of the group. He had gotten out of the service and left this kind of shit behind, or so he thought. Running his fingers around his lips tensely, he tried to keep his head on straight. *Tomorrow, you get to leave, so don't fuck it up,* he reminded himself.

Michael looked around, everything quiet. For a moment, he had a crazy thought, and he considered if the girl would be sober enough to ride, provided he could wake her. Henry wanted to get her out of this mess, maybe he could make that happen. *If she wants to go that is, otherwise we should let the Dragons keep their tainted trophy.*

Henry stepped out of the shadow, giving Michael a small start, "Hey, little brother, le's go for a walk."

Michael glanced about again anxiously and followed. When they were clear of the rooms, he eagerly shared his plan. "What if I go back and get her up, put her on my bike, and ride away with her?"

Henry shook his head while glaring at him, "If it was that simple I'd already've done it."

Their eyes locked, and Michael realized stealing Eddie's prize whore would be like asking to have his head removed. "So, I guess you just have your turn and pretend nothing's wrong with it," he spit the words out, still not able to put two and two together in the mixed up lot.

Henry shook his head, "I ain' allowed to touch her. Not since the first an' only time I've been with her." They walked a little further as he described the single night the two of them had shared, and the price he had paid for it.

Michael listened quietly, clenching his jaw, "So, if she don't wanna be here, then why is she?" *You're not gonna convince me this isn't her choice,* he added mentally.

Henry only shook his head. "I'm afraid you're on a need t' know basis, bro. I'll tell you what I can, and you'll have t' trust me on the rest. Ya see; not everything with this crew is what it looks t' be. When our service ended and we put the team together, we made some contacts. The kind you don' get rid of once you're affiliated. Ya get me?"

Michael nodded. He had been in high school when his older brother got out of the army and took on a darker, more mysterious life. Back then, he had thought he wanted to be a part of it. During his own years in the Special Forces Unit, he had a few brief encounters with Red and Eddie, along with some other members of the group. In the end, he had decided taking after his hero wasn't such a hot idea after all.

He kicked the ground in disgust, "Yeah, I get you. So you raised her, and trained her, but you won't tell me how well or what for." Henry nodded, and Michael continued with a sneer, "And you're in love with her, even though she fucks your buddies every night."

His heartless words stung. "So, are you gonna help me or not?" Henry demanded, pissed at the younger man's surliness.

Michael studied the brown eyes that matched his own. Running his fingers through his dark brown curls, he exhaled loudly, "Yeah, well, I don't really have a choice, now do I? So, what's your plan?"

"It's simple," Henry replied matter-of-factly. "You take Eddie's job an' you do it. An' you wait. When I'm able t' get her away from 'em, I'll send her to ya; I know you'll look after 'er for me. However long it takes; you gotta promise me you'll wait, an' promise me you'll take care of 'er."

Michael stared at his half-brother blankly; *that's the stupidest plan I have ever heard.* Clenching his jaw, he kept his mouth shut.

Henry looked dejected at his lack of response, "She's special, Mike. I never tol' anyone what she means t' me. But I guess you've seen more 'an I wanted you to. I'd risk everything I got an' all that I am for her."

"You know what the odds of us being successful at this are? Eddie'll kill us all if he even *thinks* we're making plans like this." Michael wasn't scared of Eddie, but he knew what the man was capable of.

Henry nodded once again. "Yeah, I know. But we gotta try. She deserves a chance, no matter th' odds."

Michael looked away, watching car lights snake along on a distant stretch of road. *Yup. This is a pretty stupid fucking plan. Gonna wind up dead, all of us.* However, as he couldn't come up with a better one, he guessed it would have to do. He turned to shake on the deal, giving his brother his word. "Ok, you get her to me and I'll see that she's looked after." After all, he would do just about anything for his brother; *even taking care of nasty whores if I have to.*

# Waiting Game

Michael sat staring at the girl as she avoided looking at him, thinking how his opinion of her had softened a bit over the years. Maybe staring at her picture so many nights and thinking about the cut on her face had something to do with that. *I still don't get why Eddie sent it to me, or why he cut her... not like she wasn't willing or anything. And I was doing my job... so why threaten me?*

Holding his tongue as long as he could, he gave her some time, but eventually there were things he needed to know. Trying not to set her off, he asked quietly, "Can you at least tell me where my brother is?"

She stiffened in the seat beside him, looking down at her hands for a long moment before turning enough to ask, "Who's your brother?"

A small chuckle escaped him, "Henry, of course. You can't tell me you didn't know. We look so much alike."

She lifted her gaze to meet him in the eye. She had suspected they were related, but had not guessed they were that close. She blinked at him slowly, her face no longer angry. It had become twisted, in a contortion of pain, and she licked her lips nervously before she began.

"I'm sorry." Her voice barely a whisper, she dropped her focus to stare at his lips as she spoke. "Eddie and Henry got into a fight, over a year ago." She swallowed, and flicked her tongue over her lips again. "Eddie was looking for

31

something, and Henry wouldn't tell him where it was. Eddie killed him and searched his body before we left him, in a field, next to the road."

Michael stared at her; his brain wasn't fully comprehending what he had heard. *Henry is dead.* A mixture of emotions cascaded over him and he snapped his gaze to the front of the bus, not wanting to look at her. He clenched his fists, thinking about the last time they had spoken.

He had been playing the waiting game about three years when the call finally came. Henry had said he had things worked out, and the girl would be coming to him shortly. Now he was sitting with her, a year later, and his brother was dead.

Michael felt the tears in his eyes, and tried to wipe them away before they fell. His brother had been his hero when he was young. The man he always wanted to be. It had been pure adulation that drove him to join the army, to go Special Forces, and to take the job watching some guy for Eddie Farrell.

It had also been his devotion that made him promise to take care of the woman who sat next to him. He nodded slowly and pushed for more, "Ok, so maybe now you can tell me how you got away from them." His voice grew anxious, "Are they looking for you? Are you in danger?"

Tori sat in silence, knowing the answers to those questions would not come easy. He watched as she took a labored breath, waiting impatiently for her to begin. She looked around nervously, not wanting her words to be overheard.

Remembering his brother's group and their use of languages, he whispered to her in German, "Whatever you prefer."

She gazed at him, surprised he knew what she was thinking. But he was Henry's brother, so of course he knew.

Grateful for the cover, she began her tale.

In a quiet tone, she explained how she had been raised in the camp by the group, and he recalled what little his brother had told him about it. Nodding, he encouraged her to go on. She continued, explaining very briefly how she had taken her place among the Dragons, skipping over all but the most essential details. Michael felt he already knew the things that mattered, and he did not pry for more.

The bus rolled along through the dark, and within a couple of hours she had shared everything that she dared with him, including the farmhouse, Chicago, and LA. Reaching the end of her story, she stared at him, her crystal blue eyes wide with anticipation of his reaction. He only nodded at the moment, letting it all sink in.

*The Dragons are dead, but The Organization lives and breathes.* Her position was precarious, and he could feel the tension in her body, aware of the danger that lay around her. He could not help but wonder how much of what she said had been true.

"So, why're we going to Denver?" he finally asked.

She explained, sounding somewhat annoyed, "I have some things I need to do there. Then I can pick a nice quiet town to hunker down in. *Alone.*" She emphasized the word alone. "I can take care of myself, and I don't need supervision. Besides, becoming involved with other people only brings unnecessary risks, both to me and to them. I can't allow that to happen."

He gathered her meaning; she had just told him to get lost. But Michael had already promised two other men he would take care of her, one of them the most important person in his life. As a man of his word, getting lost was not an option. His eyes dropped to look at her perfect pink lips. *She won't ever be your lover*, he told himself, *but you're damn sure gonna do your best to keep those promises.*

"We better get some sleep," he stated, and laid the seat back a bit to close his eyes. He could feel her watching him for several minutes, but he didn't respond. He would let her think she was in charge if that's what it took, but he knew the truth, and there was no way he would let anything happen to her; or let her get away.

A few hours later, the bus pulled into the station in Denver, and the couple gathered their things. "So, where will you go from here?" her voice sounded light and cheerful, and in an instant he knew it was an act. She wanted to know his intentions, and she was a cunning little wench. He didn't bother to reply, and simply made his way down the aisle and out the door.

Tori took a deep breath as she watched him go. Men were usually easy for her to manipulate when she put her mind to it. *Why is he being so difficult?* Throwing her bag over her shoulder, she followed and exited the bus.

Michael stood to the side, waiting for her. They were almost the same height, and she looked him easily in the eye. He nodded his head, and then turned to walk, clearly expecting her to follow.

For a moment, she thought about heading the other direction, but he paused to wait for her to catch up, and she realized it wasn't going to be that easy.

"Let's take care of your business," he spoke with calm authority, "And then we can look around for a quiet little town." He could see her eyes flash with anger.

She didn't want him coming with her, and spit her concerns at him in venomous protest. "You know, seriously, I don't need your help."

Stopping, he faced her squarely. "Look. I don't care if you want to be alone," his German perfect, "I'm coming with you and staying with you until I know you're going to be safe. I promised my brother I would do that. Honestly, I don't give a rat's ass about you. But Henry, he meant the world to me. And he loved you." He stopped abruptly, the emotion heavy in his eyes, cracking his voice.

Taking it down a notch, he continued, "So, I'm going to keep my promise to him, and make sure you're cared for. After that, I'll move on, and you can be alone." He emphasized the word alone, as she had done. He could see his words had stung her, and he knew she had feelings, even if she pretended to not care. But he wasn't going to allow himself to be manipulated by her. *I'm too smart for that.*

The two walked on without speaking, leaving the station. Making their way to a small café, they ordered breakfast and dined in an edgy quiet. Michael watched around them as they ate, half expecting to be interrupted at any moment by some new enemy that had presented itself. They remained there, drinking coffee until the sun came up. When they left the diner, he followed her to the bus stop.

Pouring over the map, she found the location she needed to visit. Standing for several minutes, the bus arrived, and they climbed aboard. Taking their seats, he realized she hadn't spoken a word to him since his outburst.

Stealing a sideways glance, he wondered if she were still pissed and how long she could keep it up. *Most women would be bursting after having gone so long without talking.*

Exiting their transport in front of a large storage facility, Michael looked at her in bewilderment. Glancing at him coldly, she directed in a curt voice, "Go inside and tell them you are Henry. This unit was his. Tell them it's been so long you forgot the number, and ask for a pair of bolt cutters in case we can't get the lock open."

He stared at her incredulously. "And when they ask for ID, what should I do then?" *stupid bitch* he added cerebrally.

"They won't," she replied flatly. Michael only nodded, unimpressed, and stomped off towards the entrance.

A few minutes later, he returned with no tools in sight. He handed her a piece of paper, "It's this way." When he had gotten inside, to his surprise, they in fact, did not ask for ID. He gave them his name, and they pulled up a black and white picture of him in their system file. Michael matched his sibling so closely, they didn't even look twice. Giving him the code for the new digital locks that had been installed, they were home free.

Tori followed him, her sneer almost gloating at her assessment of the process. He cut his eyes to glare at her, but said nothing. It occurred to him, looking after this infuriating woman would be the hardest job of his life.

Standing back, he watched her enter the code in the keypad next to the entrance, and the door began to rise on the small 5' x 5' cubical. Inside the tiny room stood several crates and boxes. Leaning forward, he pushed the lid up on one before she grabbed his arm and hissed, "Stay out of that!"

He let the lid slide back into place, but not before he recognized the contents of the dark container. Searching around for a moment, she spotted a metal tool box on the floor along the back wall. Kneeling down, she lifted the padlock on the front and peered at the keyhole. Allowing it to drop with a clang, she picked up the obviously heavy case and shuffled out into the hall. He offered to carry it for her, but only got an angry scowl in return.

Hitting the close button on the key pad, they waited for the door to be secured. Then they turned, strolled down the hall and exited the building. Taking the bus again, they made their way to a small motel, where she instructed him to get them a room.

*So much for me being in charge*, he thought to himself as he obeyed, while she waited outside. Returning with the key card, they crossed the asphalt parking lot to the correct entrance. Sliding it, he opened the door for her, and she stepped inside, placing the heavy box on the table with a thud.

The girl walked around the room, checking it anxiously. Michael pulled his jacket off and dropped it on the double bed, tired from their late night of conversation while they had ridden the bus from LA. Placing his hands on his hips, his tone sharp with disgust, "Ok, now what?"

Without a word, Tori reached inside her jacket's inner pocket and removed a lock pick kit. Opening it, she laid it on the table beside the box and selected the tools. Inserting two of the small devices, she popped the lock open in a matter of seconds, much to Michael's surprise.

Sliding the ring out of the hasp, she lifted the lid and allowed it to fall back on the table, staring down at its contents. For some reason, he had been expecting to see tools inside the tool box. What he did see took his breath away.

Reaching over slowly, he laid his hand on top of the stack of bills, his jaw hanging open in surprise. She looked at him, emotionless as ever. "Jesus Christ!" he exclaimed, his eyes darting to meet hers. "You knew this was in there?" he inquired dubiously.

"Of course," she replied calmly. "I told you that unit belonged to Henry. All of the Dragons had one; all but me. That's twelve men, twelve lockers, scattered across the country. They put stuff in there like the money, for safe keeping until we needed it. They always paid the rent for years in advance with cash, so there would be no paper trail to follow."

Michael stared at her incredulously. "Is that why there were guns in the crate?" he could not resist the question.

Tori only nodded in reply. The other crates held even more ominous equipment, but she need not go into details. However, she knew the Dragons could have easily started a small war, if the need ever arose.

Snapping the box closed, she looked around the tiny room. "This is what we came for," she stated flatly. "We should decide where we go from here."

Realizing she had clearly given this a lot of thought, Michael knew he would have to continue to defer to her leadership. *So be it.* As long as she didn't try to ditch him, he would allow her to lead the way.

Taking a seat in one of the chairs, leaning his forearms onto his knees, he looked up at her with an upturned palm, "So, what's your plan?" He listened attentively while she explained they would take the money and get on another bus.

She had been researching some locations down in Texas, and thought that might be a good place for them to head, where there was lots of open road dotted with small towns in the middle of nowhere. Besides, that put them close to the border, which also could come in handy. Nodding his agreement, he remained silent.

She further outlined how they were going to purchase a building of some sort to convert into a shop, where she intended to rebuild motorcycles for a living. He raised his eyebrow at this piece of news, not realizing she actually knew anything about them, other than riding on one.

Again, bobbing his head lightly, he found no flaw with her designs. Looking over at the container, "How much is in there?"

"$500K," she didn't even flinch when she said it.

He sat staring up at her. Her face blank, a cold chill ran down his spine. Last night, she had confessed to murdering eleven men in one night. The most fearsome group of eleven men he had ever encountered. He slowly realized, if she wanted him dead, he might not have the power to stop her.

Turning away, she announced, "I'm getting a shower."

"You just gonna leave this sitting here?" he asked in

surprise, pointing a thumb at the metal case.

Lifting her bag, she headed into the bathroom. "I'll let you keep an eye on it," she called out from the other side of the wall, and then peeked at him around the door frame, "I don't think you'll cross me. And if you do, there will be no place on earth you can hide." She closed the door, and a few minutes later he heard the water spraying lightly, and the sound of her voice as she sang in her clear, distinctive tones.

# Long Road

Michael sat listening to the girl for several minutes, running his hands through his hair while he considered the last twenty-four hours. Rising from the chair, he checked the lock on the door, then walked around to the far side of the bed and pushed it out from the wall about a foot so he could make his way down beside it.

Kicking off his boots, he stretched his tired frame out on top of the covers and allowed his eyes to close. *What the hell have I gotten myself into*? His thoughts raced.

He knew the money in the metal box was dirty. *Blood money, no doubt.* He would never touch it if he could help it. Hearing the shower cut off, he lay still, breathing deeply and pretending to be asleep. A few minutes later, the door opened and a puff of steam escaped out into the room.

The girl emerged, hair still dripping, and surveyed the space without making a sound. He expected her to take the other half of the bed to rest before they moved on. After a long silence, he could hear her breathing and realized she was asleep, but not beside him.

Sitting up, his gaze swung around anxiously. Straight in front of him stood a corner where about two foot of the wall was exposed between the small dresser and that of the bathroom. Crouching, she was leaning with her face pressed into the paint, her shoulder in the corner, sound asleep.

Michael had never seen anything like it. Lying back, he

allowed himself to doze off, his head still spinning from the chaotic turn of events.

When he awoke some hours later, the sun had almost set. The girl still sat in her corner, but faced out into the room, watching him patiently. Seeing him rise, she stood and prepared for them to leave. He noted the fresh makeup on her face and realized she had been awake long before him. *Sneaky little bitch.*

Picking up the metal tool box, she suggested they find a different case to carry it in, like a suitcase or tote bag. He had to agree that was a good idea, as it would draw far less attention. Leaving the room, they turned in the key card at the office and made their way to the bus stop.

Getting off at a large chain store, the girl sat on a bench out front with the box, instructing him to get a backpack. Staring at her for a moment, he considered if he could trust her to be there when he returned.

At his failure to move, she looked up at him, somewhat annoyed, "It's ok, you can go. I'll be here when you come out."

"And how do I know that?" he quipped, "I don't really have any collateral. And we both know you wanna get rid of me," he breathed heavily as he spoke.

Tori's jaw dropped slightly. "I didn't say I wanted to get rid of you, I said, 'I don't need you'."

"Yeah, that's it, means the same thing in my book." Not seeing a way around it, Michael marched into the florescent glow of the sales floor, half expecting her to be gone when he got back.

A few minutes later, he exited the structure, a dark blue backpack in hand. A bit surprised, he found her still seated on the bench, watching the movement of the parking lot with an unwavering glare. Standing when he approached, she met his gaze briefly before turning to lead him to their next stop.

Making their way across the street to a convenience store, Tori took all of the items into the lady's room. Michael ambled over to inspect some of the maps available on a round carousel next to the door. Finding one of Texas, he made the purchase, thinking it might come in handy for their journey, and slipped it inside his jacket's inner pocket.

A few minutes later, she returned, carrying all of the bags and box in an awkward manner. Reaching to help her, he swung her large bag over his back, and realized it carried the money. Eyeing the smaller backpack, he surmised it held her possessions and the box most likely empty. Climbing back onto the city bus, they rode to the bus terminal, and when they made their way down the aisle, she left the toolbox under the seat.

Heading into the station they had only arrived at a short sixteen hours before, they purchased tickets to Dallas. Their ride didn't leave until nearly midnight, so they made their way over to the waiting area and stretched out on a couple of benches to pass the time.

Tori tossed the pack on the bench, and then lay across it so she could keep a low profile, but still monitor the comings and goings of other passengers as they entered and exited the station. He chose a bench where he could monitor her.

Michael lay over on the bench across from her, bringing his right foot up beside him and placing the sole of his boot flat on the bench. His left foot hung off the side, and he kicked it periodically in an absent minded fashion while taking her in.

A tall girl, at least six foot, he could see she was lean and fit, too, with curves in all the right places. Blue eyes, long dark hair, but with a brooding face. If they had not met before and he learned she was a whore, he might have liked to know her.

Shifting slightly, he thought about her not having spoken

ENTWINED

to him since the bus that morning without purpose, and he began to grow uneasy about the strange girl he was now in league with. She had a keen eye, and missed nothing that went on around her. She was also strikingly beautiful, and he wondered if the picture Eddie had sent him had been faked.

But it couldn't be fake. The kid at the music store had informed him about her gruesome scar that covered her left eye. That's how he had known for sure this was the girl from his past. Watching her steadily, she suddenly looked straight at him, her eyes narrowed as if she were displeased with him, causing his stomach to do a summersault.

Laughing out loud, he stood and lumbered over next to her, triggering her to drop her feet to the ground and sit up properly on the bench. Reaching inside his jacket, he produced the map, and unfolded it. Focusing, he kept his tone civil, "So, you have any idea where you might like to look?"

She glared at him for a moment, then taking the side of the map, pulled it between them so they both could view the page. Without a word, she used a long finger to trace the line of I-20, from Fort Worth, headed west, until it hit the smaller town of Abilene. Then sliding it south, she went over the smaller highways that led between Abilene, San Angelo, and the border. Somewhere along the way, she would find where she belonged.

Nodding again he folded the map and looked at her with questioning eyes. "Don't you ever talk?" He had not meant to insult her, but her lack of conversation had begun to wear on him. "I mean, I realize we're not friends, but we don't have to be enemies, either. You can talk to me. I swear I don't bite." He smiled encouragingly, but she stared back blankly with no response.

After a moment, she broke her eye contact and leaned back away from him to watch the doors again. Clearing his throat nervously, he tucked the map back inside his jacket and stood up to walk around, realizing this would be a long road if she continued her icy disposition.

When the time came, the couple climbed onto the bus, each of them putting their bags under their seat before sitting. Again, Tori sat on the inside with the window to her left, which Michael found a comfortable position, as he could observe her more easily without drawing suspicion.

Removing her jacket, she spread it across her lap, and he could see the collection of scars that dotted her right arm as it brushed against his. Peering down at it, he made out the remains of what once had been cuts, scratches, and perhaps even cigarette burns on her skin. He also noticed the tone of her muscles; *definitely fit*.

His gaze slid a little to the left, and he could see down her shirt. After a moment, he realized he was looking at the spot where the bite mark had been on her left breast. He had, more or less, forgotten about it until it wasn't visible, having gotten a good look at it the night Red had fucked her.

Studying the location, he could trace the outline of the makeup that she used to cover the eyesore. He considered her reasons for doing so briefly before he raised his gaze to find her staring at him as he gaped at her cleavage. Her face like stone, Michael could feel the flush rising up his neck as he had been flat busted ogling her breasts.

Turning his eyes back to the front of the bus, he shifted anxiously in his seat, and they rode in that fashion for several minutes. Feeling uneasy and a need to explain himself, he finally glanced back and forth between her angry eyes and the road ahead.

"You know," he began softly, "I never actually touched you that night. That night you were with Red." He paused for a moment, not sure how else to describe it. "You passed out after he finished with you, so I covered you with a blanket and left you there." He looked down at his hands, pressing the palms together nervously, waiting for her to process the news.

"Why didn't you?" she asked, her voice quiet, innocent.

He looked back at her and could see her eyes were wide with disbelief. All of a sudden, he couldn't tell her the truth. He hadn't touched her because she was dirty; a whore. Michael had only been with two women in his life, and he had loved them both. Somehow, he didn't think knowing this would make the girl next to him feel any better, so he lied.

"I just didn't want to." He shrugged for effect. "I'm not really into that whole, nasty sex thing, you know?" He let the words drop with a nod, hoping he had spared her feelings. He hadn't. She knew exactly what he meant.

Turning back to the window, she scowled into the darkness. She didn't care if he looked down her shirt. He had chosen not to touch her, and she liked that. *I don't wanna be touched anyways, and if he ever changes his mind, I'll kill him.*

# Small Towns

The couple scarcely spoke to one another as they worked their way from Dallas to Fort Worth. They had decided to do a bit of shopping, as Michael had no possessions with him other than the clothes on his back and a dead cell phone. Purchasing another backpack, he filled it with two changes of clothes, a package of cotton briefs and a bag of socks.

Tori approved of his choices, telling him noncommittally, "At least you can travel light."

Her words made him smile for a moment, but he felt odd when he realized this. *Yeah, like I need your blessing,* he mentally challenged her, wiping the tiny grin away for good measure.

Boarding another bus, they made the short ride to Abilene in the middle of the day, arriving before dinner time. Eating at a small local dive, she announced they would pick up some bedrolls and hike the rest of the way south.

Late in the year, fall was setting in, but the warm climate had been one of the reasons Tori chose Texas for making her home. It didn't get very cold down south, and if it did, it didn't last long. Having grown up in temperate Brazil, this was important to her, and Michael agreed with her logic.

They spent the night at another motel, enjoying showers and repacking their gear more evenly between them. He tried to take the lion's share of the load, but Tori wouldn't have it.

"I can carry my own weight," she insisted in a cross tone.

He got the impression she only had two moods; angry and pissed. *Why she didn't ditch me when she had the chance is beyond me,* as she obviously didn't like him, or anyone for that matter. *She's a damned enigma.*

Studying her while she rearranged her pack, it occurred to him she may have worked out a plot for him. *Something to use me for.* He knew she was deceitful and would never let on what her plan was without a purpose.

He was discovering winning arguments with her was damn near impossible as well, as she was easily the most stubborn woman he had ever met. Preparing for the night, he chirped in a cheerful voice, "You take the bed; I'll take the floor." He lost that argument also, and felt a bit put out about it as they settled down to rest.

Lying in the dark, he could make out the outline of her back as she crouched in the corner. He could tell from her breathing she had fallen asleep. *Man, I don't get this bitch. Or what the hell Henry, or anyone else for that matter, ever saw in her. She never speaks without a reason, never just talks. She never smiles either, unless she has something up her sleeve.*

Rolling onto his back, he covered his face with his hands, and then pulled them down to stare at the ceiling. Tomorrow, they would hike out of Abilene and head south, down the state highway. And he would have to listen to her silence. *God, it's maddening.* Soon, Michael drifted off to sleep as well, his mind still restless as he dreamt.

When he awoke the next morning, Tori was already dressed and washing her hands, having applied her makeup first thing. By then, he had seen the scar on her face, and he had to admit, it was pretty gruesome. He still carried the picture in his wallet; the one Eddie had sent him after he cut up her face. However, he didn't let on that he had it, or that he knew about the scar before he actually saw it.

Watching her as she moved about the room, preparing to leave, an idea crept into his circle of thoughts; *Henry loved her, and that's all that matters. I need to accept that fact... and her; get on with the task at hand. Henry would have wanted it that way, and I can be professional about this.* Pushing the memories aside, he got dressed and also prepared his things to depart.

When they were ready, they collected their new packs, which consisted of a blue foam bedroll and a light sleeping bag each. The money had been divided between them, along with their clothes. This would make the going a lot easier, and they picked up a jug of water for each to drink as they moved. A few granola bars and a bag of dried fruit and they had what they needed to survive from town to town.

Michael wasn't really sure if she would be able to live like that for long. He had never known a woman who could truly rough it. *She lived with the Dragons, but that was different,* he recalled, *as we're on foot and at the mercy of the elements.* He fully expected her to fold.

They ate that morning at a small café next to the motel with another extended period of silence, but Michael endured it. He noticed Tori ate eggs and bacon, and drank three glasses of water, while her eyes kept watch around them, constantly moving. He had decided she moved like a scared animal; calm, but always alert.

Leaving the register, she picked up a cap from the counter and smiling, purchased it. He noticed the tiny grin, and turned the cap where he could see the words *Real Bitch* stitched in white letters across the black material. Shaking his head, he didn't say a word, knowing it would only start a fight if he did.

Making their way down the side of the road, Tori donned her new cap with pride. "You know," he eventually called from behind, "We might get a ride from someone if you weren't wearing that stupid thing." She slowed her step to let him catch up and fell in beside him.

"Now why would we want to do that?" she inquired in her quiet voice, but he noticed that she smiled again, a little more broadly this time.

"Because *you* never talk," he answered, not looking at her and his irritation beginning to show.

Tori shot him a look of surprise. Trudging along, she nodded at him, and then stated emphatically, "If the quiet bothers you so damn much, you talk. I never said I wouldn't listen."

Michael wondered how she managed to make him feel foolish so often. They walked quietly for a short while longer before he relented, "Ok, then I guess I will. What do you want to know?"

Tori shrugged, turning her palms to the sky and spreading her hands wide, "Anything… Everything." Her smile said she meant it.

Michael started with his brother, Henry. He told her how they shared the same mother, who had remarried after Henry's father died in a car accident. "Basically, the woman had two families," he explained, "As Henry was already fifteen when I was born and out of the house by the time I started school."

He decided not to mention that his own birth had been an accident and that Henry had been the only person on earth that made him feel like he was ever wanted. Instead, he shared how he had always adored his big brother, and would have done anything for him. He could see the wistful look on her face as she listened, giving him confidence to continue.

He told her about his job with *Indelible*, making sure they would be safe everywhere they went. He explained that he had enjoyed the work, and she seemed interested in the idea of preventing someone from getting hurt rather than causing it, a real switch for her. Michael smiled, admitting it had been a real switch for him, as well.

Eventually, their pace slowed, as the conversation became more balanced between them. He then realized she had plenty to say; only it took her longer to get it out, especially where Henry was concerned. He had always known his brother had loved the girl. Listening to her talk about him, he strongly suspected the feeling had been mutual.

The sun moved high in the sky as they ambled along, and eventually they stopped to break out snacks and have a good drink of water. In the distance, they could see a small group of buildings ahead, and figured they would make it before nightfall.

"I hope there's a place to eat," he muttered in a low voice.

"No worries," she countered with a hint of mystery. "If there isn't, I'll show you how to catch a rattlesnake and cook it."

He stared at her in disbelief, noting she grinned from ear to ear as she tossed her pack on her back and headed off without him. He shook his head to himself; *she has got to be kidding*, but deep down he feared that she wasn't.

"I know how to catch a snake if I want to," he sounded irritated as he caught up to her, "I'd just rather *not* need a ride to the hospital because you thought it'd be cute to show off your snake hunting skills."

She looked at him sideways, trying to decide if he were picking on her; his tone said that he wasn't. "Not all women need a man around to take care of them, you know," she bit out curtly and quickened her pace once again.

*Ah great. Now I'll get the silent treatment again;* Michael chastised himself. *Fucking bitch.* But he deserved it, and he knew it.

They did reach the buildings, but it turned out to be a group of houses and barns, no other structures in sight. The pair kept moving, and as the sun sank low, they started watching for a spot they could put down their bedrolls for the night. Luck was with them, and they came upon a small abandoned shack that stood a bit off the road.

The sun moving to set, they climbed over the barbed-wire fence and headed towards it. Taking a look around, Michael realized they were not the first to make camp there, and found a fire pit on the back side, complete with a section of expanded metal to lay over the top. Gathering up a few bits of mesquite, they would be able to build a small fire.

In the fading light, Michael busied himself by poking around inside the gutted structure. It had been a small shed, probably for tools or a bunkhouse back in the day. It had wood and brick walls, and the roof made of rusted tin. One might have hidden inside, but due to the fear of having the assembly cave in on them, they opted for the ground instead.

Michael set up their bedrolls next to the fire pit. While he worked, he noticed that Tori had disappeared, and for a moment, a stab of panic gripped his chest and he spun around, scanning across the horizon wildly, until he saw her a short distance away. She appeared to be rummaging around a fairly large pile of rocks. His stomach growling, he pulled out the bag of dried fruit to munch on while he headed across the loose soil to meet her.

As he got to her, the girl stood up, and he could hear the rattles shaking in a loud flurry. "Oh, shit!" he exclaimed when he saw the creature hanging from her hand, almost dragging the ground as she held the diamond back out at about eye level.

Shoving the bag of morsels into his pocket, he reached out to help her, but she quickly sank to her knees as the knife in her other hand extended with a loud pop.

Placing the head of the snake against a rock, she made a clean slice with the blade, removing the business end of the creature about four or five inches down the neck. The body of the serpent dropped, writhing about wildly on the ground, and she held the cranium carefully to avoid either of them coming in contact with the fangs.

Michael stared at her, his face stoic as he realized she had been successful, almost making it look easy. Tori looked up at him for a moment, giving him a toothy grin. Collecting her prize, she carried both the body and the snout back to the small shack.

Dropping the lengthy portion on the ground, she left it to finish its spasm of death, while she found a spot and dug a small hole to bury the mouth portion, not wanting anyone to be stabbed with one of the fangs, which still held their venom.

Michael's heart pounded forcefully in his chest, but she appeared perfectly calm as she set about collecting suitable wood and grass to use for building their fire. He had seen such things many times, but not performed by a woman, and that fact completely unnerved him.

Michael had never really seen a woman as his equal, as they always needed something, and were never quite independent of the men around them. Henry had asked him to take care of her, but he had begun to wonder if she really needed him to, as so far she had come across as pretty resourceful.

Following her, they worked until dark, at which time he realized they would have no light to work by. Tori seemed unaffected by the drop in visibility, and after they returned to the small camp with their supply of sticks and branches, skinned the long snake easily in the early night. Sitting back on his bedroll, Michael sufficed himself to watch her. He noted she wasn't the least bit squeamish, the realization bringing with it a smile.

Tori's hands moved expertly over the long body as she cut off the poop end and pulled away the guts from the inside. They came out easily, in a long strip, and she inspected the length of the snake briefly before sectioning it. Giving him a quick glance, he could see the sparkle in her eyes as she asked if he knew how to make a fire.

"Of course I do, I'm a man, remember?" Michael felt a little irritated as he put the materials down and used the matches to set the dried grass tinder ablaze. The thin strips of mesquite caught fire easily, and Tori skewered the strips of snake to hang them over the flames using small Y shaped sticks as leaning posts.

She had placed a small Ziploc of seasonings in her bag, such as salt, pepper and cayenne, and they sprinkled their preferences on a few strips for each of them. Sitting back in the cool evening air, they watched the flickering tendrils as their meal cooked. Gazing at her face in the dancing light, Michael found himself in awe. *She's really different.*

"How do you know all this?" he finally asked, trying not to sound condescending.

Tori sat with her knees pulled to her chest and her feet flat on the ground in front of her. Her arms were wrapped around her legs tightly, and she rested her chin on the tops of her knees, watching the fire.

Giving him a small shrug, she eventually replied, "I grew up in the jungle. Literally. I lived there with the Dragons about fifteen years that I remember - who knows how long before that. And the rest of my life, I've been on the road. This's normal to me."

He had begun to understand her quiet ways, and decided to leave her alone as they sat in the dark together, enjoying the smoke and the smell of the cooking flesh.

After the snake finished baking, they pulled the tender

bits off that ran along the backbone, and ate the tasty bites. "Anaconda is my favorite," Tori blurted out unexpectedly.

Michael's lips broke into a wide grin at the thought of her catching and cooking giant snakes in the amazon. She seemed so much more relaxed, and he felt pleased to see her that way. She was talking a little more, but she still seemed very guarded. *She don't trust you,* he warned himself, *even if you are Henry's brother.*

Having finished their meal, they spread their sleeping bags out on top of their blue foam rolls. Sliding off his boots and standing them up, he watched as she did the same, well aware of what might like to make a home in them.

Inside their bags, the couple lay with their heads only a few inches apart. The highway lay a few hundred yards away, and only rarely did a car pass by as the hour had grown late. The darkness became peaceful around them.

Peering up at the night sky, Michael considered how she lay down, and could not resist the temptation to ask, "How's it you're stretched out here, but when you sleep in a motel, you cower in the corner?" He waited patiently for her to percolate her response, becoming accustomed to her thoughtful pauses.

"I guess it's the walls," she offered softly. "I don't really like walls."

He had to admit, it sounded feasible. Out there, the sky expanded above them, and the clear blackness was strewn with stars. He had loved camping with his father when he was a kid, going to lakes and such, the few times his old man had had time for it. It surprised him that she wasn't as averse to roughing it as he had thought she would be.

Thinking back, he realized he hadn't seen his father since his mother died, eight years ago. He had been in the service at the time, and only went home long enough to bury her. When he got out, he never bothered to go back, as he had never really been close to his father, or anyone else for that matter.

*Hell, the old man may not even be alive any more.* The only person who had ever mattered was Henry, who was gone now. Michael released a deep sigh; *guess I really am alone in the world.*

Thinking about what his brother had told him about the girl, Michael decided to see what her version would be. "So," he tried to be casual, "How is it you ended up in the jungle with a group of street thugs? I mean, what about your parents?" He waited again, and after the pause became longer than most, he turned so he could see the top of her head, the breeze gently rustling her dark hair.

"I don't know my parents," she admitted, her voice barely audible. "I don't know who I am. No one does. The Dragons raised me, and I killed them, and that's all there is to the story."

Gazing back over at the fire pit, Michael doubted he had heard the entire tale, but this wasn't really the time to push for more.

Drifting off to sleep, the night passed without incident, and the two awoke with the sun. Packing up their gear, they made sure the fire was completely dead before walking away. Picking their way back through the sparse foliage to the road, they crossed back over the spine covered fence.

Several times, Tori stopped to inspect a variety of the cactus they came across, and he finally asked what she was doing. Without looking up, she said calmly, "Observing them." She pulled out her spiral bound notebook and made notes about the latest one.

Internally, she had become excited at the prospect of studying plants adapted to live in a dry desert climate, also known as C-4 vegetation, as her previous life had been focused on the opposite, rainforest type C-3 greenery. They were designated as such by the type of photosynthesis they used to produce their food.

Scowling at her current specimen, she knew her companion would not understand her fascination with learning about them. She was beginning to see he was nothing like the man who had cared for her when she was a child, even if they did share the same mother, eyes and hair.

Michael wasn't sure how to take her sometimes. Trying to remain calm, he asked why she was bothering to do that, and again she made him feel foolish when she replied, "Because it's good to know your environment. We're not far from potential locations for the shop, and I want to know what I can about the local habitat if I'm going to live here."

"And why would you care about that?" he asked in a less diplomatic tone.

Standing, she averted her eyes as she walked past him, tossing over her shoulder, "Because Henry taught me to."

Continuing south, they made it to a small settlement shortly after noon. Tori took the opportunity to freshen up in the diner bathroom, and Michael pulled out their map to assess their progress. When she returned, they ate in silence, his unhappiness with her generally unimproved.

On the road again shortly thereafter, they made it on down the highway in a slow procession of days, nights and small towns. If they found one big enough for a motel, they pulled in for the night for showers, and a good meal, but otherwise, they were pretty comfortable as they traveled at a slow, steady pace, eating off the land or what small provisions they carried.

Michael began to wonder exactly how she planned on choosing the place they were looking for, as she did not seem to have one picked out by name. Whenever he would ask, she would simply say, "I'll know it when I see it."

The third time he asked, she stopped to look him square

in the face, "If you don't like it, go away."

He didn't like it, but he wasn't leaving either, so he only wrinkled his nose in disgust and kept walking. *My God, she's infuriating.* He wondered if she were wandering around like that in an attempt to run him off.

He had noticed she did not refresh her makeup after the first motel in Abilene, and had washed it away completely in the first diner where they had eaten. *Perhaps another attempt to scare me away. Good luck with that, crazy bitch.*

Two weeks later, he had become fully accustomed to looking at her scar, and hardly noticed it, especially when she smiled. He noted that she smiled more often when they were away from people, and questioned how much of it was due to that separation from everyone else, or if she were actually getting used to him.

A few days later, they did find it. They had come upon yet another small town with a diner, and had sat down by the window to enjoy their meal, when she whispered quite loudly, "Oh, my God, there it is!"

She pointed out of the large glass for him, and, by turning and looking over his shoulder, he could see an old gas station two short blocks away, on the opposite side of the main street. The pumps were gone, and all the glass was boarded up, but the walls were still standing, and that could be called a plus.

Finishing their food, and with the girl obviously excited, the two of them scurried down the street to look the place over. Tori grinned from ear to ear as she walked around the building and inspected the back area, where a smaller building stood, the windows also boarded up. The garage's structure had concrete running all the way across the front, and a large storage shed attached to the back side of it that needed paint. It was perfect.

The small assembly behind clearly a housing unit of

some kind, it stood long and narrow, running across the back edge of the property; at maybe twenty feet deep, and fifty foot wide along the front. Trying to peer in through the holes in the plywood that covered the windows, it appeared pitch black inside.

Making another trip around, the roof appeared sound, and the weeds were kept down around the two structures, creating a small yard area about one-third of the lot in square footage. Tori was obviously pleased.

Michael did not feel so enthusiastic, but he decided he wasn't going to argue. *It's her money, and I'm tired of hiking with her anyways.* Dropping his gear on the ground, he leaned against a tree and waited for her to make her inspection. Watching her as she flitted about, he found himself curious about her level of obvious excitement.

As he surveyed the lot, he noticed there was no real estate sign posted, and grew concerned that they might not be able to acquire the property. Collecting her, he suggested they go back to the diner and start making their enquiries there to see if they could find out who owned it. Otherwise, they could go over to the courthouse and look at the tax records. Either way, it would be a place to start.

# Hidden Treasure

Back at the diner, Michael saw a woman named Trish, by her nametag, working feverishly behind the counter cleaning glasses. Leaving Tori by the door, as she still stared down the road at her hidden treasure, he made his way over to the middle aged woman to inquire about the property. Being a small town, it seemed highly likely she would know who owned it.

Breaking into a broad, friendly grin, she exclaimed in a thick southern drawl, "O' course I do. It belongs t' my father-in-law, bless his heart. He had a stroke a few years ago and had t' retire. The place has been sittin' there empty ever since." She went on for several minutes before he cut in and inquired whether or not it was actually for sale.

Michael nodded as the hefty woman continued on again, "So you two are inner'sted in buyin' the ol' place? I could give you his address; you can go right over an' talk t' him about it. They live in an ol' house jus' a couple o' blocks over." He quickly agreed, and she drew him a small map on a page from her ticket book. Tearing it out to hand it to him, she continued talking about the building.

Walking to the door, he heard the woman call after him, "Ya'll head on over an' I'll call right now an' let him know you're on your way. Jus' ask fur George." The glass door closed and he realized the woman was still going on, and for a moment he felt very appreciative of his much quieter companion, but he wasn't about to tell her that.

They made their way around the café to head in the opposite direction, crossing the street and walking a couple of blocks. Finding the old Victorian style dwelling easily, Michael skipped up the steps to knock on the peeling white paint of the screen door.

Tori stood out in the grass, looking up at the sad old house, suddenly homesick for LA. Staring at the rickety swing on the porch, she thought of Max and the talks they had shared on a swing like it. With a deep sigh, she hoped he was doing well.

When he rushed back to her excitedly, Michael could have sworn for a moment she had wiped away tears, but she smiled weakly, "What did they say?"

Unexplainable butterflies filled his stomach, "We need to go inside so we can make the old man an offer."

Stepping up onto the porch, Tori snatched the Bitch cap from her head. A slightly round, older woman held the screen door open for them. She told them they could drop their bags outside if they wanted, but giving each other a quick look, they agreed they would rather not and carried them inside. They placed the packs on the bottom step of the stairs that stood about six foot in, and aligned with the front door.

The interior of the house appeared as old and run down as the outside. Michael looked around, thinking there wasn't anything less than twenty years old to be seen. There stood a large old television that probably still had tubes inside it against the wall formed by the stairs. All of the furniture looked to be from the 1970's, and the fixtures appeared original to the house.

On the far side of the room stood an archway that led into the dining room and further on into the kitchen, only he saw no table. Instead, there stood what appeared to be a hospital bed, probably the only modern item on the premises.

60

Glancing over at Tori, he could see her taking it all in. In German, he warned her to let him do the talking, and she silently gave a small nod to agree.

Tori took a seat on the outdated couch with little claw feet while she continued to peer around. Michael sat down next to her, so close their legs brushed briefly before he scooted away, giving her some space. An old man sat in the chair to her right, next to the upright piano that stood against the exterior wall, between two very large windows covered by brown lacy curtains or drapes that had once been white.

Michael could see the oxygen tubes running from his nose to the small machine sitting on the floor, and inferred the bed in the dining room meant he probably could not climb the stairs. Swallowing hard, he tried not to stare, his eyes shifting around anxiously. *Wow, he's on his last leg,* Michael deduced about the emaciated gentleman in plaid pajamas.

The older woman sat down on the piano bench, which stood next to her husband's chair, and Michael took the opportunity to introduce them, "I'm Michael... Anderson," he stated warmly, "And this," he indicated the girl next to him, "This is Tori. We're here about your building. Trish told us you own it, and we're hoping it might be for sale."

Marge smiled and introduced herself, while George looked back and forth between the two of them for a moment, his gaze dropping to inspect their hands. Then in a low raspy voice, which held the same thick southern accent his wife had used, "The station don't make money like it used to." It appeared he wanted to warn them that making a living in the small town selling gas and repairing cars would be extremely difficult.

Tori sat quietly next to him, allowing Michael to continue the negotiation, who explained in a calm voice, "We don't actually want to use it as a gas station; we want to turn it into a repair shop for rebuilding motorcycles."

Immediately, the woman shot up from her perch, protesting loudly, "You can't put a shop like that in our town! There'd be hoodlums in and out o' here at all hours o' the day an' night."

Michael was taken aback by her sharp words, and sat speechless for a moment, not sure how to respond to that argument.

Quietly, Tori spoke up, adopting a soft southern drawl that matched the locals. "We don' wanna fix 'em fur other people. We wanna buy old uns and repair 'em. Sell 'em at shops in the big city. There won' be nobody comin' here for our shop. No one'll ever even know it's here."

Michael gaped at her sideways as she spoke. He would have been surprised, except hardly anything about her surprised him, she seemed so unlike other people.

Staring at George, her eyes were pleading, crystal blue orbs of hope as her bottom lip protruded into a perfect pink pout. She could feel their chances of getting their building growing slim, and she made her desperate attempt to charm him into selling.

George gazed at her for several minutes before stating, "We want fi'ty thousand, in cash." He spoke with great effort, the oxygen still hissing in his nose.

Michael nodded calmly, "We'll have it for you by tomorrow. When can we meet to sign the papers?" They came to the agreement they would meet the next afternoon at 3:00 pm, down at the courthouse.

Tori and Michael would bring the cash, and George and Marge would sign over the deed to the property, including the small house in the back. Marge did not look very happy about the arrangement, but Michael suspected she would feel better once they had the money in their hands, pretty sure the amount far more than the property was actually worth.

Leaving the house, the pair tried to remain calm, but inside Tori felt ecstatic. Michael could see the spring in her step, and caught up in her elation, reached over to give her a quick squeeze. However, as he moved closer to her, she abruptly backed away, her happy expression replaced by something darker, not allowing him to touch her.

"What," he challenged with a playful laugh, "I can't give you a hug?"

Trying to regain her composure, she said simply, "I don't like to be touched," and turned to head back to the diner at a quickened pace.

Michael followed her with almost angry short strides, watching the way her rear end swayed below the ends of her long dark waves. *What the fuck? Don't like to be touched... what is that all about?* He grumbled bitterly to himself the entire way. Looking around the tiny seating area, he dropped into German to keep their conversation private.

"So, what do you mean you don't like to be touched?" he demanded as he reclaimed his seat across from her. "You used to have men touch you all the time, suddenly you don't like it? Or is it just because *I* wanted to touch you?" He emphasized the word *I* for her by slapping his chest with his fist to make his meaning clearer.

Tori stared down at her hands, which were trembling. Drawing a deep breath, she looked up into his creamy brown orbs, considering his words for a moment.

"I never had a choice; I let them touch me because they hurt me less if I was submissive. If I tried to fight them, they still got what they wanted, and it hurt a lot more. I can say no now, and no, I don't like to be touched." The tear that had been building spilled over, and she caught it with her hand as it streaked down her cheek, swiping it away with a quick, irritated motion.

Michael sat staring at her, blinking blankly as he

considered what a strange combination she was, always pretending to be so tough, when on the inside so soft. He frowned slightly as he thought how he would have said she acted more like a man than a woman in so many ways. Of course, she had been around men her entire life; and surely that could be the cause. Sitting in the heavy silence, he felt a little guilty at always being so short with her.

Looking around the café to avoid staring at her, he took note of its layout, and considered how it was a central part of the small community, as the locals came and went continually. It had a glass front from booth level to the ceiling, where the door stood in the middle, with five dark blue leather booths on each side. There were booths down the walls towards the back, another five deep. The two front corners held large round tables where groups of old men gathered in the early mornings and had done so for years.

Coming in through the front doors, there lay a bright white counter that made a square to the left, with short stools around it. Trish spent most of her time in the bar area, as many of the community members chose to sit at one of the six blue upholstered seats that lined each of the three sides.

The back wall behind the counter held the pass-through window to the kitchen in the back. The orders hung there to the left, on a large silver ring with metal clips, and a group of coffee pots and tea machines ran along the counter underneath the long window. The actual door to the back stood on the left, in the back corner where he ascertained the office area lay, as well.

To the right of the entrance a jigsaw of tables congregated, four chairs each. These were movable, so they could be pushed together for larger parties, with a few two seat tables along the back wall where the hall to the bathrooms could be found. A simple design, probably one they had seen half a dozen times in their weeks together already. The constant coming and going of people reassured him, in fact, they had discovered the heart of the town.

After he had taken it all in, Michael calmly glanced back at his companion. She had recovered from her momentary show of emotion and sat once again wearing her face of stone, staring down the road at their soon to be property. Noticing a slight twitch in her left eye, he mentally traced the outline of her scar, and his mind returned to their conversation about her being touched and her activities with the Dragons. *I guess Henry was right after all; it was all an act... I never would've believed that.*

At that moment, Trish came over to refill their water glasses, and Michael inquired, "Say, you guys have a bed and breakfast or a motel in town?" He knew a hot shower would do his cohort good, as he had learned at least that much about her.

Of course, Trish knew just the spot, as a small, four room motel could be located nearby, and she gave them the directions, along with a history of the place. Listening to her, he suspected she had been in the town a very long time, as she seemed to know everything about it.

Thanking her whole heartedly, they set out again, and a short walk later came up to the small establishment that lay beyond their small gas station. Having seen a larger portion of the tiny metropolis, Michael felt glad it wasn't so miniscule it didn't have at least some amenities.

Besides a courthouse, it held a business district that housed a small supermarket, hardware store, post office and bank. The variety shop, next to the supermarket, had clothes and household goods, so a great deal of items were available, but not a lot of choices in color or style for them. These things would come in handy at only six blocks from the station, since they did not have any type of vehicle for moving supplies as of yet.

Going inside to get their room, Michael could see the back of Tori's head as she stood outside the glass panes. She had her back squarely to him, and he thought her dark waves looked really pretty in the fading light. Her arms were crossed, and he could see her hugging herself tightly, as if she were cold. Picking up the key, he wondered if she ever got lonely, keeping everyone away like she did.

Michael led her to their room and let her have the first shower. The room itself spacious, compared to others they had spent the night in, they settled in for the night. It had a small kitchenette along the left hand wall as you entered, with a table that sat against the front window to the left of the door.

The bathroom and vanity area in the back had a larger closet attached to it, with a queen sized bed along the right hand wall, nightstands on both sides. It functioned more like an efficiency apartment, and might make a nice place for them for several weeks while they worked on getting the house in order if she would allow it.

Taking his shirt off, he lay on the bed waiting, hearing her muffled voice as she sang in short bursts. He thought about the song she had sung back at the music store in LA before everything went haywire. He guessed, almost certain, that she had written the melody. It fit too closely to what he knew about her life to have been composed by anyone else. Nobody's Angel. *She don't like having people around her; that's for sure.*

He tried, with some difficulty, to remember the words while he waited. When she exited the bathroom, drying her hair, she didn't look at him. Instead, she made her way over and sat on the end of the bed, facing the door to his left with her back to him.

"I want to thank you for helping me get here." Her voice sounded small. "I really appreciate your assistance." The towel crumpled in her lap, she sat without moving while she stared at the exit, her shoulders slumped.

Michael drew his breath in slowly. If he were not mistaken, a fight was coming on. "Yeah, no problem, right? I told you I was gonna look after you, didn't I?" He tried to keep his voice steady, but he could tell by the droop of her body she wasn't in a good mood.

Sitting up straight, she swung her damp head around and turned to look at him over her left shoulder, so that her scar glared at him, "I want you to leave after we buy the building tomorrow." She paused for a moment and then ploughed on. "I'll give you half of the money, the half that you've been carrying, if you'll just go. Go, and don't ever come back."

Michael stared at her, his mind turning slowly. "You know, I think we need to talk about this," he stated calmly, pulling himself up from his reclined position, "And this is not the time."

Standing, he went into the bathroom and shut the door. Turning, he rested his forehead against it. His heart pounded heavily in his chest as he raised his right hand and let it press flat against the wooden surface.

His thoughts were scattered in a dozen directions. Drawing deep breaths, he tried to compose himself and think. In the end, he knew he could not force her to let him stay. *It's her money.* Money his brother had probably left for her to rebuild her life. *There's no way I'm gonna take any of it, even if she offers it to me.*

Slowly removing his pants and briefs, Michael stepped into the shower. He let the water wash over him, picking up the bar of soap, still wet where she had left it in a small tray. He imagined her using it to wash herself. It made his stomach feel funny, thinking about it gliding over her scarred skin, lathering her womanly curves.

He used the soap on his tired muscles, and allowed his

mind to picture her soft flesh. He had seen her naked. He had watched other men take her; men he thought she wanted. If he had been of a mind to, he could have had her himself. The thought flashed into his mind; *thank God I never touched her, not if she felt she had no choice!* He would never force himself on a woman; he wasn't that kind of man.

Shutting off the water, Michael found another towel and slowly dried himself. Realizing he had not brought any clothes into the steamy cubicle, he briefly considered putting on the briefs he had pulled off. *Fuck it*, he thought as he wrapped the towel around his waist and strutted out into the coolness of the room, the light growing dim as the sun had begun to set outside.

Looking around, he found her leaning into the corner, as she always did. She rested against the wall and cabinet in the kitchen area facing the front, with the bed to her left. Leaning closer, her eyes were closed, and he judged from her breathing, to be asleep, so he dropped the towel and tossed his bag up onto the bed to rummage inside for some clean underwear.

Pulling on the fresh cotton, he slid them up and then turning, realized she was staring at him, her face expressionless. Running his fingers through his wet hair, he suddenly felt ashamed of himself and what he'd been thinking. Grabbing his clean pants, he hoisted those on, too.

Walking over in front of her, he flopped down onto the floor and sat cross-legged, facing her. "Please don't make me leave." His voice cracked slightly, and he covered his mouth with his right hand, clearing his throat a few times into a slight fist.

Drawing in a deep breath, he continued. "I'm not ready to go yet. I realize I can be a real jerk sometimes." He paused, noticing she lifted her chin as he spoke. Nodding his head, he tried again, "What I mean to say is, I know I can be a real asshole. A lot of the time. But I don't mean to be. And if you'd see fit to allow me to stay... I swear I won't ever touch you, unless you want me to, and I'll do my best to treat you better."

He searched her features for any sign of what she thought. After what seemed an eternity, she nodded slowly, and turned to put her face back into the corner. Watching her, he breathed a sigh of relief. Standing, he pushed his bag back onto the floor and stretched out across the bed. Sleep loomed a long way off that night, as he had started to see the girl who shared his space in a different light, and his head ran in circles.

Michael could hear as her breathing changed into a sleeping rhythm. Rolling onto his side, he could see the outline of her in the dark. He had discovered so much about her. *No wonder Henry had loved her*. She needed him, but she wasn't needy. In fact, more like the opposite, and getting close to her would be the challenge.

# New Beginnings

When they got moving the next morning, neither of them mentioned the night before, but it weighed heavily in the air. Michael watched her, wondering if she felt any better after having a good night's sleep. He reminded himself he held concern because his brother wanted him to look after her, and that's what he intended to do, but deep down he had begun to have a hard time selling that line, even to himself.

Together, they counted out the $50K and put it into one of the backpacks where they could pull it out easily. Then, Tori counted out an extra $10K and placed it in another pocket that could also be easily reached, just in case. When they were set, they went to check out of the small suite and made their way over to the diner for brunch.

Of course, Trish greeted them warmly. Tori had put her makeup on, and the woman surprised her by commenting quite loudly about it. "Oh, hun; you got yur makeup on today, got that ol' nasty scar o' yours covered. It looks really nice, let me tell you." She was friendly in the oddest ways.

Tori stared at the woman as if she had fallen out of a tree, and Michael could not suppress his laughter at the girl. Seeing her cut him an equally dirty look, he tried to quell the spasms, using the back of his hand, and then his white linen napkin. Eventually, his jovial outburst subsided, and he wiped the tears from his eyes before they brimmed over and ran down his cheeks.

"I'm sorry. I'm sorry," he stated between quick, deep breaths, "You're so darn cute, I could not help myself." She stared at him blankly but did not comment on his backwards compliment.

Michael regained his composure and looked over the menu briefly before they ordered a good meal. He had noticed she ate the same foods he did and today it occurred to him that he had started a kind of tally on her. How she measured up, so to speak. Why he measured her, or what for, he still wasn't sure.

Sitting quietly again, Michael used their covert language, German, to discuss plans for the shop with her. "You know," he started out, "We need to make a list first thing of all the repairs that're going to be needed, on the building and on the house. That way we can get that stuff taken care of right away before winter gets here, in case we do get any bad weather."

"I know how to run a business," she snapped.

Michael stopped moving in mid drink, staring at her for a moment. "I never said that you didn't," he spoke quietly, returning his glass to the table.

Tori looked down at her lap and said nothing else.

The silence became stretched as their meal arrived, and their shyness had continued. They ate their food quietly, Michael thinking about how he could make things better. *She don't like it when you help her. What the fuck am I supposed to do?* Images of the way the Dragons had treated her flashed before his eyes, and he knew he wasn't about to be like them.

Leaving a generous tip on the table, the pair walked down to the garage and weaved around the grounds, trying to see in wherever they could. It occurred to him that they may have been a bit hasty making the purchase without seeing the inside. *No way in hell I'm gonna say that to her.*

Michael watched her as she made her way around, but

71

rather than looking at the building, she checked out the trees. They were mesquites, quite tall and fine. She had her hand on one of the trunks, staring up into the canopy, a reflective expression on her face.

Drawing a deep breath for courage, Michael quietly inquired, "So, what're you thinking about?"

Tori cut her eyes over at him for a moment and then back up at the tree. After a few minutes, she replied, "I was thinking about the bush camp, and my pink trumpet tree." Then, after another pause, she inquired, "Have you ever been there?"

Shuffling closer to her, he replied in a low voice, "Nope. Never seen it. In fact," he continued, a little more confidently, "I've been trying to imagine it ever since I met you. Would you mind telling me about it?" his words were soft, and he leaned against the tree next to her as if he had all day to wait.

She stared at him blankly, considering his request. Then she began talking about the trees, the plants, the water, and the animals. She described habitats and hunting, the camp layout and the seasonal changes. She had talked for over an hour before she finally stated, "You know, you can stop me when you've heard enough."

Michael smiled back at her, "Not a chance." His reply made her lips curl just enough, and they were comfortable together again.

Gazing over at the building, she nodded, "Yeah, we need to get a list going. Looks like we'll have a long one." Shifting her eyes back to him, she could see his smile grow larger at her observation.

At two o'clock, the couple crossed the street and headed for the courthouse. They both were growing weary of carrying around everything they owned, and as if in silent agreement, the house would be renovated first.

George and Marge arrived right on time, although the older woman still looked rather unhappy about the sale. Michael noticed that she gave Tori a dirty look, and he wished he could reach out and touch her, to let her know he was there.

The situation caused an odd thought to pop into his mind. He speculated how hard it must have been for his brother, being forbidden to touch her. Considering that he had loved her, it could be viewed a form of torture. *Knowing Eddie Farrell, it was probably meant to be.*

It only took fifteen minutes for the transaction to take place. Michael pulled the cash out of his bag and handed it over with a smile. Tori had to produce the tiny card she carried in her wallet that established her emancipation before she could fill out the paperwork for the deed transfer.

Glaring down at it, Michael noticed the name Farrell on the card and felt a stab of anger at the idea, "Kept Eddie's name, huh?"

"Yeah," she explained quietly, "It was the only name they had, and it wasn't changed on the committee's say so."

He placed another tally mark on his invisible board for her.

As soon as they were finished, George handed Michael the keys, telling him if they needed anything they knew where to find them. Michael took note of the bright smile Tori wore when they left the stone structure. He felt a twinge of guilt, remembering his conclusion about her only smiling as a deceptive device, as she clearly appeared happy at the moment.

Making a quick stop to get the utilities started, they were informed it would be three days to get the electricity turned on, but the water would be working in a few minutes, as they would send their guy over immediately.

Tori seemed a bit put out, but Michael reassured her it

would only be a minor setback. Thinking about the efficiency suites, he mentioned them in a reserved tone, "You know, we could always crash over at the motel while we work on the house if need be."

"Naw, I think we'll be fine, we have a yard after all." She smiled again, enough to make his heart flutter for a moment.

Arriving back at the property to make a shopping list, they walked hurriedly, heading straight to the back where the apartment stood. Unlocking the door and stepping inside, they took in the simplicity of the floor plan. The door opened into the kitchen, with a living area off to the right, the two only separated by the texture of the flooring. On the far wall, a hallway exited the kitchen to the left and led to the back of the dwelling.

Taking the small passage, they found it opened into a small utility area, with a back door on the right, and washer and dryer connections straight ahead. Light filtered in through the covered windows, allowing barely enough to see the large space, the linoleum floor torn and useless.

From the hallway, he could turn and face the smaller bedroom that aligned with the back door, only 9' x 9' plus a tiny closet. When facing the smaller bedroom, the furnace would be on his left, directly next to the entrance of the bedroom.

Next to the smaller bedroom, to the right, stood the only bathroom. It had to be quite small, with a sink, toilet, and shower tub combo cramped inside; the details were hard to make out in the low light, but the smell hinted at heavy repair work ahead.

Beside that, the other bedroom door lay facing the hallway he had come in from. The larger bedroom of the two, it contained a walk-in closet and room for a larger bed and more personal items, taking the entire end of the house.

Looking at the choices, Michael and Tori both pointed at

the smaller bedroom and chimed simultaneously, "I'll take that one."

Staring at one another for a moment, they began to laugh out loud, and he found himself pleased to hear the sound. He could barely make out her features in the murky glow, other than her straight white teeth.

"It's your house; you should get the master bedroom," he insisted.

"I sleep in the corner, and therefore I don't need room for a bed."

Her words brought Michael up short, as he wanted to continue the debate, but at the same time, he didn't want to upset her. Rubbing his lips for a moment, he finally agreed half-heartedly.

"Well, I for one hope you can someday sleep in a bed, and don't need corners anymore." He looked her square in the face in the floating dust as he spoke, earnestness weighing heavy in his voice.

"Ok," Tori replied softly, "I get the smaller room, and when I'm ready to sleep in a bed we can switch." She honestly thought that day would never come, but it pacified Michael, as he liked the way it implied he would not be leaving anytime soon.

With the room arrangements settled, they were faced with one fact: they had a lot of work to do. Dirt coated everything, and the carpets would all have to be removed and replaced. There were a few pieces of furniture, but most likely they were trash. Some of the walls were damaged and would have to be replaced before they could be painted; a few windows needed work or to be replaced, and cabinets refinished or replaced.

Tori looked around, loath to confess she had little experience with carpentry and household affairs, but Michael already suspected as much. They had previously discussed the need to make most, if not all, of the repairs themselves, and were mentally preparing for the weeks of work that lay ahead of them to make the house livable.

Walking the short distance to the local store, they loaded up two shopping carts full of supplies, including candles for the first few nights with no power. Michael picked out many of the tools they were going to need, while at the same time trying to keep from upsetting her at the amount of work that lay ahead of them. He thought to himself with a wry grin; *we're gonna need to eat this elephant one bite at a time.*

During the first outing, they were also able to get a few household necessities, such as a few towels. They discovered that the color selection was sparse in the small shop, and so they ended up with shades of brown and green for most everything. Surprisingly, the girl did not seem bothered by this, and Michael found himself wondering if she didn't care, or if she actually liked the deep earth tones.

While they were there, Tori stopped to inspect their selection of plates and other dishes, but they would wait to purchase those when the cabinets were ready. He liked the way she had already begun making plans for the future, and seemed to be settling in right from the start. The girl was easy to please, and she got another tally mark during the shopping.

They looked like regular vagabonds, pushing the carts towards their new home. She confessed to him that she really didn't know a whole lot about living in a house. "I learned a few things, I guess, in the halfway house back in LA. But it's kind of daunting, thinking about actually doing all of this on my own."

"Well then, I guess I'll teach you. And in exchange, you can teach me about motorcycles." He had ridden for years, but certainly wasn't a mechanic by any stretch of the imagination. His eyes dropped to gaze at her soft pink lips as he spoke, aware of the smile that curled on his own.

With a cautious look on her face, she seemed to consider his offer carefully before accepting it. Everything was new to her, and she obviously still had issues with trust, so he tried not to let it bother him, or to push her too far, too fast.

That night, while darkness crept into the small space, they lit some of the candles and placed them around the living area that stood in the front of the house. Spreading out their pallets and sleeping bags, they created their camp inside on the floor. Tori lay on hers for a moment, but he could see her eyeing the corner.

Michael rolled over to face her, and talked to her in a soothing voice, focused on keeping the conversation going for as long as he could. "I need to clean out that shed pretty quick."

They had peeked inside, and discerned that the plethora of car parts would be of little use to them, and otherwise could be pulled out and disposed of, leaving a fine storage space for the new tools they would be purchasing to work on their new home.

"Mmhmm," she answered in a quiet tone. "I wish there had been some real tools in there."

Michael chuckled, "I see, the tools that qualify as real are the ones you use on your bikes."

Tori ignored his comment, her voice growing quieter, "Maybe there will be some when we open the shop. However, I suspect anything of value was sold off or removed when they sealed the buildings."

He could hear her energy level dropping as she spoke, and he played along until she finally drifted off, lying on the pallet.

Watching her as she slept, he liked the way the flickering flame of the candles danced across her face. *She has such delicate features, and with the scar hidden by her lying on it... she's really a pretty girl.* Putting them out, he stretched out and studied the ceiling in the quiet until he fell asleep, as well.

The next morning, she lay staring at the dirt coated paint above her when he awoke and inquired, "So, how'd you sleep?"

"On my side mostly," she replied in a flat tone, "But a bit on my back."

Michael chuckled, "I never figured you for a sense of humor."

"Yeah, well, I wasn't really trying to be funny." She stood up and began to put her boots on, ready to get on with their day.

Joining her, Michael felt a tingle in his palms, excitement at the realization that she accepted his being around and shared her space with him. *And she made a joke. Well, I think it was a joke.* Either way, she was becoming comfortable, and he liked that, even if she tried to pretend it wasn't true.

Over the last few days, he had been forming a plan for building their relationship in the back of his mind, and he knew he would have to take it slow if it were going to work. He wanted them to have a new beginning; a place for them where they could each belong and have a new and better life.

Up until that point, he had been acting on his word, the promises he made to his brother and to Terry. Now he was forced to admit his motives were not so altruistic. In fact, a spark had begun to glow inside his heart. It had been small, but growing larger, faster than he could control, it warmed his spirit towards the girl so unlike any other.

He feared saying the words yet, even to himself, but deep down, he knew what was going on. Watching her while they walked towards the café to get breakfast, he had a quiet revelation. *You like her. Really like her,* he thought with a sheepish smile. Taking a seat at their regular table, he could see the sour look on her soft lips, and wondered what she was thinking. *You can't change her past; you know. You have to take her as she is.*

Noticing how she avoided looking at him, he realized her history seemed less important to him. It made his heart pound when he thought about it; *I don't really care who she was with. Or how many times. Or even why.* He kept his smile hidden, the freedom his thoughts afforded him staggering.

Their plates on the table, he further noted that he had accepted that she really had no blame in the things he had witnessed so long ago, and felt somewhat guilty about all the names he had called her. *Thank God I never said any of those things out loud!* He wrestled with the idea that she had picked up on the vibe, even if he hadn't, and hoped she would forgive him.

*She's not really to blame for what happened to her, and didn't deserve to be judged so harshly. She's a strong woman, willing and able to take care of business, no matter how hard or unsavory it might be.* He wondered if she felt the guilt that those darker choices could bring, and he admired her for her courage to make that stand.

In a way, this realization gave him resolve to make things right for her if he could. Watching her as they ate that first day as true members of the community, he made a quiet promise to himself; *I'm gonna do my best to give her the life she deserves.* Not because he had given his word to anyone else that he would. He would do it because he wanted to.

# Everything Is Fine

Back at their newly acquired property, the couple cleaned out the shed. It was a good way to pass the time until the house had electricity, when they would have some light to work by. Michael set up the small space for the tools he had purchased, and felt pleased when she allowed him to give her a lesson on how some of them were used. He noticed she remained quiet, but attentive, and he had begun to read her moods more easily by the time the truck pulled up to set their meter.

Once they had power, Michael and Tori went to work on the house in earnest. From the very first project, he set about teaching her some carpentry and masonry during the remodel. He became impressed at how quickly she learned and her willingness to try whatever he asked of her. He was definitely in charge, as the expert, and she accepted it without argument, making an excellent student.

They started with the bathroom, as the room that they needed most urgently. The tiny rotted cabinet beneath the sink had to be cleared out before a new one could be installed. They had to do some heavy cleaning on the porcelain surfaces, as the hard water stains and buildup were tremendous.

Eventually, Tori suggested they should purchase a new toilet and sink, and they resurfaced the bath tub, so it looked new again, as well. Michael felt pleased with the outcome, and she smiled in her shy way when he praised her choices. He noticed she did, in fact, have a fondness for dark earth tones, which he also found calming. He thought about the tally marks, as she had so many by then, and tacked one on for this, as well.

The bathroom in order, she put a soft mat down on the bare concrete floor to cover it until they were ready to lay the tile. She also hung the plain towels on the racks, and he noticed that she stood in the doorway and stared into the tiny room for a long time. He became mildly curious about her thoughts, noting she spent a great deal of time reflecting. He had quickly realized asking only seemed to prompt a foul mood, so he left well enough alone, knowing she would share when she felt ready.

They had electricity, but the water heater was shot. Michael longed for a decent shower, rather than the cold water spritzes they had been using to refresh themselves since they moved in. She got another tally mark for her good nature, as he could tell the lack of facilities bothered her as well, but she never complained. He liked that she took things in stride.

Since they had been in the house a week, Michael persuaded her to make a trip to the motel that evening to have a real shower and refresh themselves a bit. He had thought they might spend the night in the comfortable room, but once she had cleaned herself, Tori expressed a desire to go home. He silently agreed, as she slept on her mat without argument, and he wanted to continue the headway she was making.

Strolling through the dark to their small work in progress, they discussed the purchase of the water heater. He took the opportunity to pitch their need for a washer and dryer unit as well, "If we get them now, it'll add a little convenience to our schedule. You know, work smarter, not harder." He smiled encouragingly, but noticed she wore a stoic expression.

"But we're not finished with the floor," she protested.

"Naw, it's ok though, we can pull them outside when it's time to lay the tile. Until then, at least we'll be able to do laundry without so much hassle." He gave her a sideways glance as he made his case, knowing she didn't like to be pushed.

Tori only sighed in response, keeping her thoughts to herself.

They made it back to their haven, and she wandered to the back of the house to survey their work and the laundry area before bed. When she returned to the living area, she found he had laid out her bedding for her, and she stretched out across it to stare at the ceiling, wishing he would stop doing things for her; *I can take care of myself*, she thought almost angrily.

"You know, I'm not domesticated," she made her point bluntly, irritated with the man next to her.

"Yeah, I got that," he agreed, "But it's not a bad thing. You just have to decide it's something you want. Or which parts you want. However you care to put it." He glanced over at her and smiled; *at least she's able to think about having a normal life.*

Without taking her eyes off the ceiling above her, she sighed, "Ok, well, we can get the laundry room stuff then. But don't expect me to be washing your clothes or anything."

Michael snorted a laugh, "Yeah, listen. I'm a big boy. I can do that kinda stuff for myself. No worries." He watched her, a little disappointed she didn't return his gaze, noting she had actually turned her back on him to stare at the wall. Exhaling loudly, he rolled to face the other one. *Small steps, but at least we're moving.*

The next morning warranted a trip to the hardware store,

where they were able to pick out a washer and dryer from the small selection they had on hand, and they were delivered later that afternoon. At the same time, they ordered a water heater to be installed a few days later. They needed one that would fit in the small space, and decided to opt for a tank free model that would mean an endless supply of hot water.

Tori refused to admit it, but she felt more relaxed after she gained the ability to have a hot shower when she wanted one. She also became comfortable taking up her morning workouts, which were a great release for her frustrations. Michael made free to join her a few times a week, and she chose not to make a scene about it, even though she would've preferred that she have that time alone.

As everything in the house seemed to need something, the couple spent endless hours working side by side, and Tori found herself chatting with him more as talking eased the boredom. Deep down, these endless days wore on her nerves, as she still felt plagued by the idea that he shouldn't be there, and she would need to find a way to get rid of him, sooner or later.

Michael, however, liked her company and the fact she seemed to be enjoying his, as well. He had reached the point of almost seeing the two of them as friends. They had so much more in common than he had first suspected, and were finding peace in their interactions, albeit he discovered he had to watch himself most of the time to maintain it.

He wondered if she felt the same way, but had learned that asking direct questions was less effective with this elusive female who seemed more guarded than anyone he had ever known. He had to take care, allowing her to come to him in many ways, so he did not push her to explain herself or how she felt about things.

Having the bathroom completed, the couple began work on the kitchen. He showed her how to strip the cabinets and apply new stain. Michael liked the way her face became tense when she focused on doing a good job at something, like applying the thin layers of pigment on the wooden doors. They had chosen a deep mahogany, and were able to find a small table to match that had deep green legs and chairs.

They purchased black for the oven and fridge, and she commented offhandedly that fire was a much healthier way to cook as she refused the installation of a microwave. She watched patiently while he hooked up the lines to the stove and a trip to the local grocery was in order.

They stocked the small pantry that stood next to the hallway with cooking materials, but Tori insisted most things needed to be fresh rather than processed. This meant the grocery store became a near daily adventure as well, and Michael noted that she seemed to take comfort in having a pattern to their days, almost like a strict routine that threw her off when things were done out of the allotted time slot.

Tori felt somewhat eager to try her hand at cooking their first meal in their new place. Visibly disappointed at the result, her roommate reassured her it would get easier with practice. She stared at him as he ate the meal hungrily, as he had no intentions of hurting her feelings by complaining. She took his actions as a type of deception, and wondered if he was actually scared of pissing her off.

That night, they rolled out the sleeping pads, as usual, and she stretched out on hers comfortably. Watching her, Michael felt a familiar ache in his chest, glad they were working on the common areas first. *This way, she's having time to get used to sleeping on the pad until her bedroom is complete*. By the time they were ready for beds, he hoped she would be able to move into one. *It's practically the same thing, and if I have to, I'll put the mattress on the floor and move it onto a stand later*.

"What're you thinking about?" Tori's voice cut sharply

through his conniving. He lay staring at her profile, deciding how to respond. Rolling onto her side, she glared straight at him. "Don't lie to me, either," her poor attempt at dinner and his inability to call a spade a spade fresh in her mind, she felt ready to throw a fit at the first hint of deception.

Michael's face grew pale, as he contemplated her suspicion of him. "What do you think I'm thinking about?" he tried to turn the tables.

Rotating onto her back again, she glowered at the ceiling, "I want to work on the shop. I'm tired of messing with the house."

He sighed in relief, "Yeah, actually I was thinking the same thing." He lied smoothly, and Tori seemed content with his acquiescence.

As had become the norm, she turned her back to him and faced the large glass window that stood in the front of the house. He could tell something bothered her, but once again, he avoided making an issue over her idiosyncrasies.

Michael lay watching her breathe, her dark curls shimmering in the moonlight that shone in and lay across her body. He sighed deeply, hearing the steady inhale and exhale that meant she had fallen asleep. *I may be in over my head here, but I can't let it go.* The thought sifted through his mind as he, too, drifted off to dream land, fighting the urge to reach out and touch her as she slept.

The next morning, he woke up early to find the house empty, and surmised she was off for her workout. He pulled his clothes on and made his way outside, where he found her doing stretches on a small patch of still green grass under her favorite tree. Trying to appear calm as he sauntered up to her, he squatted down next to the tree and inquired nonchalantly, "So, what're we up to this morning?"

"Don't you recognize exercise when you see it?" she asked in a mocking tone.

"Ha, Ha," he countered. He had been up with her several times to train, but had quickly learned she was much more hard-core about it than he was. At the moment, he felt content to watch, not able to take his eyes off of the spandex as it hugged the contour of her rear end when she bent over.

For a split second, she caught him gawking before he tore his eyes away. Straightening slowly, she glared at him for a long moment. "Is something going on?" He gave her a purely innocent stare. "I'm serious, Michael. You're really scaring me."

His eyes grew wide at her words, and he stood up from where he had been crouching next to the tree. Tossing his head back and raising his chin towards her in a challenge, he countered, "What am I doing that scares you?"

Her face became wrinkled in a strange expression of confusion, "I don't know. You make me feel all weird, like you're watching me, but you're not watching me. And you're nice to me, which doesn't feel right."

It was his turn to be confused. *How can someone being nice not feel right? Does she really expect me not to be, especially since I promised to treat her better?* Michael sidled closer to her, "And?"

"And that's it. Something about you doesn't feel right."

He moved to stand very close to her, not touching her, but definitely in her space. He could hear the change in her breathing, and he half expected her to back away. He shifted his gaze from her pure blue eyes to her perfect pink lips and back again. "Everything's fine, baby girl," he tried to comfort her.

"Don't call me that!" she objected loudly. He raised an eyebrow in question, and she continued angrily. "That was Henry's name for me. I don't want you to use it. You," she huffed loudly, "Are not Henry." She shook her head, a tremor in her voice.

86

Michael smiled, confident they had hit upon the problem. "You still miss him, don't you?" he asked the question with a flat tone, like a statement.

She glared at him for a long moment. "I don't know. He's been gone a long time. And even when he was alive, we weren't permitted to be close to each other. It's almost like he died..." she trailed off, unable to finish, but he knew what she meant.

Henry had told him long ago about the one night they had shared and how special it had been to him. He felt confident it had been special to her, too. Abruptly ending the conversation, Michael stomped back to the house, unwilling to fight with her and wishing he didn't look so much like a dead man.

# Lost Loves

After a shower and breakfast, they cracked open the shop and started poking around. Upon entering, Michael commented that they should have opened it first and stayed in there, as it was in much better condition than the small cottage. The windows were boarded, but intact, and the walls only needed paint. If the tools had still been inside, it would have been almost perfect.

They discovered the roll up door needed to be replaced, so they made a trip to the small hardware store to place an order to have one delivered and installed. During the outing, Tori seemed especially quiet and even more standoffish than usual, as if she were trying to keep him away. Michael blamed their heated conversation that morning, and tried not to reignite the debate.

By the time they arrived home, he felt exhausted with preserving the peace between them.  She cooked a surprisingly very tasty dinner, and he grinned while he devoured it. "This is fantastic," he breathed airily, but she only stared at him in return.

Michael rocked his jaw side to side as he studied her. "Hasn't anyone ever given you a compliment before?" He hoped his tone wasn't too angry or condescending. However, he had grown weary of dancing around her past life, and felt ready to clear things up, before they choked on it.

Tori shrugged, her eyes roaming between her half eaten

meal and her newest roommate's rugged features, "I guess they have, but it's hard to take them as sincere," she practically called him a liar to his face. "I wasn't exactly raised by a nice group of men, you know; and the ones I've known since then weren't any more trustworthy in the end."

Her voice trailed away, feeling a little guilty for lumping him and Henry in with all the rest so out of hand. Besides, there had been more than a few in LA who had genuinely cared for her, and she had chosen to put them behind her for their safety, not because they were unworthy of her friendship or trust.

Nodding slowly while stabbing meat on his plate, "I get it," Michael agreed. "I used to think I was pretty alone in the world myself. I mean, Henry was pretty much my only family. With him gone, you're just about the only friend I've got."

Tori sat wide eyed, not having realized they had become friends until he pointed it out. Swallowing hard, she wasn't sure what to say next. Opening her mouth, she muttered an inaudible comment about friends coming few and far between. She then stared at her plate, unable to eat another bite, her stomach in knots.

Deciding he had pushed her enough, he let the conversation fade and finished the delicious meal. *She's turned out to be one hell of a cook, even if she can't stand to hear it. Not domesticated... whatever she tells herself,* he thought to himself with an inward chuckle. As he finished cleaning his plate, she surprised him by reopening the discussion.

"Would you like to hear about them?" she spoke at a whisper.

Michael chewed his last bite slowly, "About who?"

"About them. The men I was involved with. There have only been two, besides your brother. I don't count any of the ones…" her voice trailed away again.

Her proposal sounded odd, and he considered it for a moment, wondering what her motive for sharing the tales could be. Giving her a small nod, he braced himself for whatever she was going to throw at him.

Upon his agreement, Tori took a deep breath and began with Eli, then moved on to Enrique. It took her less than half an hour to tell him everything she could remember and that she was willing to share, about both men, combined. As she finished, Tori quietly admitted, "I didn't actually love either of them. I mean, I thought so at the time; when I was with them. But I know better now."

Michael's heart began to pound, *she knows better now, huh,* "What makes you think you didn't love them? You had sex with them, obviously you felt something for them, in order to allow them to touch you." He waited patiently for her to get her story straight.

"Because I can't remember them," her explanation simple. "I try to think about them, but there's nothing there, other than the sex. Like they didn't really exist, or I didn't really know them. They could have been anyone. It's kind of like the drinking. I did it because it's what I had always done, like a habit. Not because I loved them or should have been with them. No more, no less. I've reached the point I don't even believe in love."

Her words shocked him, and he frowned, "You know you loved Henry. You have to know that." Shaking her head, she avoided looking at him, and he could tell she had grown uncomfortable again and sat in silence for several minutes while he waited for her to continue.

Finally, after a lengthy pause, she admitted in a submissive tone, "Henry meant a great deal to me, but he was at least twenty-five years older than me. Our relationship wouldn't ever have been normal, even if we had somehow been able to leave the Dragons and make a life together. I think that's why he wanted to send me away. To someone else."

"You mean to me," he stated flatly.

Tori stared at him, a shocked expression crossing her features, "I mean you what?"

"You mean to me. Henry, he intended to send you… to me."

Breathing in short pants, she realized he was right. Henry had made him promise to take care of her, and obviously did intend for the two of them to be together. Her brow furrowed, "Surely he didn't think we would be a couple."

Michael pushed the bare plate away and folded his hands in front of him to lean on his elbows. "Who knows what the man thought? The only thing we can be certain of is, I have fulfilled my promise to him." He smiled, hoping she understood how important that fact was to him.

She met his gaze, her expression thoughtful as she continued, "You know, I was almost twenty when he and I were together. However, I was raised in the camp, so I never learned any of the things most boys and girls learn early on about relationships. Physically, I may have been grown, but emotionally, I don't think so. I never had any real peers; I guess you could say, and I've been stuck somewhere… not a child, but not really a grown up either."

Michael nodded again, "Yeah, I can see how you might feel that way. There are lots of things everyone takes for granted; things you haven't experienced yet. That doesn't make you a child; it just means you have a different perspective. Besides, you act like you're the only person to have lost at love. I assure you, you're not."

Tori smiled slightly at his playful grin, "I suppose you're here to nurse a broken heart?"

He chuckled lightly. *Well shit. Look where we are now. If*

*I tell her, this could be a disaster, and if I don't, I look like an asshole.* Running his fingers through his sandy brown curls, he knew he didn't really have a choice, so he used a low tone to explain, "Well, I have only loved two girls in my life... The only two women I have ever been with." He avoided looking at her, not wanting to appear that he was judging her.

Shifting, he tried to look more comfortable than he felt, "The first was my high school sweetheart, and we were pretty hot for each other back in the day. When I went into the army, she said she would wait for me. But, a year later, I got a letter from her. Said she was having a baby with some other guy. She had moved on after I left, but never bothered to tell me about it." He had been devastated, his face covered in the pain he didn't have the words to convey.

"The second time happened while I was stationed overseas, and it ended when I came home to the States. She refused to come with me, saying that if I loved her, I would stay with her in Germany. I wasn't going to do that, so I broke it off clean and never looked back."

It didn't sound very clean to Tori as she noticed the hurt in his eyes. She stared at him as he talked about them, feeling sad that they both had endured such agony in the name of love. "So that's it, then? If you want to avoid getting hurt, you have to stay away from people?" She smiled to herself, realizing that had been her plan all along.

"Not at all," he countered quickly, meeting her gaze. "Love is worth it, no matter the outcome. I mean, when it ends, it's gonna hurt, whether you had thirty days or thirty years. But the joy of that time... it's completely unbeatable."

"Oh, my God, you're a romantic!" she laughed out loud at him, in awe that he could sound so tender; she had known few men whom she would ever give such a label, and fought the urge to make fun at him for his weakness.

Michael nodded his agreement. "I guess in a way I am. But I rather consider myself a realist. This world isn't perfect; we aren't perfect. Life... will never be perfect. Remember that. The choices we make, dictate the lives we lead, Ba..." he cut the words off, almost using the forbidden nickname.

Tori smiled at his slip, knowing he didn't mean anything by it. Feeling like they had exhausted the subject, she sat and stared at him in awkward silence. *So, he's not a womanizer. He deserves a real lady.* She held his gaze, a little sad that she would never qualify for his short list of true loves. *All for the better, as his days in this house are numbered.*

Michael returned her glare; *yeah, this was a topic we should have avoided, at least for now.* The quiet palpable for several minutes afterwards, each of them became lost in thought.

Eventually, the couple cleaned up from their dinner. It was getting late in the year, and Michael wanted to light the furnace so it would come on when it got too cold inside the small structure. "We're gonna need some beds soon," he commented absently as she stood watching over his shoulder. "Make sure we stay warm at night."

Tori got an odd look on her face at his statement, and he felt like they had had enough awkward conversations for one day. Cupping his hand over his mouth in an exaggerated manner, "You know what? I think we need to get some sleep." The furnace set, he replaced the cover, and headed into the living area to roll out his mat and flop down on it.

Tori stayed in the laundry room for several minutes before she finally joined him on the floor, lying on her mat. He could not help but wonder what she had been thinking, even if he felt too terrified to ask. Things were moving fast for him, and he didn't want to spook her if he could avoid it. However, she seemed to be coming around, and he liked the idea of making his next move, now that he was getting an idea of what it might be.

The following morning, Michael got up early and slipped over to the café. Finding Trish, he asked her a simple question, "Where's the closest jewelry store?"

Then he sat down at the counter to listen to her talk for five minutes before she finally got to the part he needed, "About twenty miles from here."

Standing, he walked around the small dining area, asking if anyone was headed over that day or any time soon so he could catch a ride. Watching him with a giggle, she finally called him back to her, "Why don' you jus' take my car? You can drive can't you?"

He stared at her in disbelief, "You'd really let me borrow your car?"

"Sure, hun," she gave him a huge grin, "But really you two kids need t' get a car o' your own if you're gonna be livin' way out here in the middle o' nowhere like this."

Michael wasted no time in disagreeing with her, and then asked for her keys and where he could find it. Holding up the ring of shiny metal, "Out back, hun. Buick Skylark."

"Trish, you're a doll! If Tori comes looking for me, tell her I had to run an errand and I'll be back soon." Obviously excited about his mission, he jogged out the glass door and made his way around to the alley.

But Tori wasn't going to go looking for him. She had heard him leave the house and still felt weary over their conversation the night before. *He's growing too eager to be close to me. What the hell was I thinking, telling him about Eli and Enrique?* She hadn't told him everything, but she had told him enough. She got up and went right to work, trying to do something productive for her house that would eat away at her nervous energy, her thoughts in turmoil.

Deep down, she had a new fear growing inside her. She

had begun to like having him there, and becoming too comfortable with their friendship; she cringed at the word. *This's exactly what I wanted to avoid. Having people close to me is dangerous.* Soon, she would have to decide what she was going to do about it, and either accept his being there, or run him the hell off once and for all.

# Small Surprise

Michael didn't waste any time getting over to the next town, and it didn't take him long to find the jewelry store Trish had described. Gazing up and down the old buildings that lined the street, he felt comforted by the simple style of the smaller community and the depth of its personality; so different than the impersonal shopping malls and centers of big cities.

They were unlocking the doors when he arrived, and he could not have felt better going in. He walked around peering down into the glass covered cases, thinking he should have been nervous; he wasn't. As if for the first time in his life, he knew exactly what he needed. *It's not time yet, but I'm gonna be ready when it comes*, he smiled as he moved.

Finding the large expanse of engagement rings, he slowed down to take his time. There were so many, but mostly too big, gaudy even. *Tori isn't like this. She's simple, quiet, plain.* Seeing the polished wedding bands, his heart began to thump loudly in his chest. The clerk who had been hovering close by became eager to help.

"I need two of these in white gold. One that fits me, and one that fits," he paused, not sure what to call her, "A girl."

The salesman looked down his nose, "And what size is your girl?"

Michael felt stuck, because he had no idea.

Thinking for a moment, he came up with a plan. "Let me

pay for the rings. I'll find a sneaky way to get her size and call you with it. We live in another town, so I'll have to pick it up later anyways. And I want it engraved." Michael grinned, overjoyed with his idea.

Sliding his digit into the finger sizer to measure it, they finished the order. Leaving the store, he hummed to himself, and Tori's song sprang into his head. She had called herself Nobody's Angel, but she was wrong. She had become his angel, even if he didn't have the courage to tell her yet. He had thought of her as devious, but he could play that game as well.

Reaching the car, Michael noticed a small music store across the street, not unlike the one she had worked at in LA. Looking both ways before he crossed, his palms were sweaty as he leapt up onto the sidewalk on the other side.

Peering in through the glass, he could see the row of guitars along the back wall, as well as the expanse of other instruments littering the small space. He had never intended to spend so much of the money they had pulled out of Henry's vault; the blood money. But he could not help rationalizing it, as this was for her. He hated to admit he had reached the point he would do just about anything for his dark haired beauty.

Tugging to open the glass door, a bell rang, and an older man with long hair came out. Michael chuckled to himself at the similarities between him and Terry. A stab of guilt panged his heart, knowing Tori had left, and everyone who cared about her had no idea how well she was doing. *Well, everyone else who cares.*

Not knowing anything about guitars, he understood this would be more difficult than the ring. He began to talk to the old man, who explained about the basic parts, such as the bridges, strings and pickups, and Michael did his best to listen. He had worked for the band for over four years, but never bothered to learn anything about the instruments that they played.

Eventually, he decided to pick a really nice looking one and get a good amp. "Can we bring it back if she doesn't like it?" The shop owner agreed that as long as they brought it back within a reasonable amount of time and undamaged, he would exchange it.

Michael chose a black and white model; colors that seemed to suit her. He also got what the salesman called a decent amp and a case to go with the guitar, along with wires to hook it all up. Loading the items in the trunk of the car, he thought he was all set, when he noticed the flower shop next to the jewelry store.

Shaking his head slightly, he didn't bother to suppress his grin, *might as well go for broke, right*? Inside, he purchased an arrangement of pink roses, and the lady gave him a box to put the vase down in so it wouldn't fall over while he drove and cause any of the delicate stems to be broken.

The short trip home, Michael became a bundle of nerves. He had planned a small surprise, but realized he had much more than that. His hands gripped the wheel with excitement, and he kept repositioning his tingling fingers. Pulling up behind the diner, he grabbed the box with the vase of flowers and carried it inside.

Catching Trish, he returned her keys and explained the hidden contents of the trunk, his enthusiasm unsurpassable, "Is there some way you could put it up for me until I'm ready to surprise her with it?"

Trish agreed, eyeing the large bundle of roses. "You sure are sweet on that girl," she told him with a grin.

Michael could only smile as he confessed, "Yeah, well, I really am beginning to think the same thing."

Sliding the vase out and leaving the box at the diner, he made his way down the street, gingerly carrying the large offering out in front of him. When he arrived, Tori was kneeling on the floor in the back part of the house, preparing it for the new tile. Quietly placing the large bouquet on their tiny kitchen table, he made his way down the hall in stealth mode, his steps not making a sound.

Standing in the narrow hallway, he admired the view, as her rear end faced him and wiggled nicely while she worked. His smile faded away when he heard the distinctive sound of a sniff, and realized she was crying. The awareness paralyzed him for a moment; he stood still, like a stick of wood. She sat back onto her heels and twisted to look at him.

The sight of her eyes swollen and red, the path of the tears on her cheek, took his breath away. After a moment of staring at one another, he breathed a single word, "Hi."

Rising, she dropped her tools into the bucket beside her and shifted into the little bathroom to wash her face and make herself presentable.

Michael stood and watched her as she did so, afraid to take his eyes off of her for a moment. After she had steadied herself, ashamed she had been caught blubbering, she managed a weak smile and her own, "Hi" escaped her pink lips.

This brought a huge smile to Michael's face as he backed down the narrow hall, not wanting to turn his back on her. "I have a small surprise for you," he spoke in a low, wistful voice. Stepping into the kitchen, he continued to back up, turning down in front of the fridge and stopping in the corner created by the sink and the oven so that her view of the table was unobstructed.

Her eyes grew wide at the magnificent display, and she covered her gaping mouth with her right hand as she considered what to do. Finally, Michael could not wait any longer, and asked, "So, do you like them?"

Staring at him, she considered what accepting them

would mean. Finally, she made up her mind, knowing what had to be done. "Why did you bring me flowers?" she asked quietly. Her question made him uncomfortable, and he shrugged while he tried to remain calm. "Michael, you know you can't stay here."

Her words stung, and he continued to smile, although it felt strained.

Shaking her head, she went on. "I only let you come here until I was settled. That's what you said; you would stay until you were sure I was ok, and then you would leave me alone." She tried to keep her voice steady as she spoke. "I think it may be time for you to go."

Michael felt like he'd been stomped. *This's not how I pictured this working out.* "Can't you just accept that I did something nice for you? Do you always have to assume there's a sinister meaning behind it?" He tried to keep the quiver from his voice that would give his hurt away.

Shaking her head slowly, she spoke barely above a whisper, "Michael, I can't accept these. I mean, they're beautiful, but roses are for people who love each other, and I already told you, I don't believe in love. I don't believe I'm *capable* of love."

He stared at her, jaw clenched, the smile completely gone, and not really trusting what he had heard. *Not capable of love. Who the hell isn't able to love someone?* Shaking his head, he tried to persuade her she was wrong, but she wasn't having it, so he half turned away, and faced the far wall in the end of the house.

"We need a deadline. How many more days do you want to stay?" she asked the question as if she were ordering pizza and needed a list of toppings.

"I don't wanna leave," he tried to be honest, turning his head to look at her with a sideways stare.

"Not good enough." Tori shook her head, "You tell me

when, or I'll choose the date for you."

Michael drew a deep breath, his mind drifting to his other purchases. He knew he could make her love him, but he would need time. "What's the longest you will give me?" he asked quietly. "May I stay until spring?"

Closing her eyes for a moment, Tori realized spring lay a long time in the future, as it was still a few weeks until Christmas. "When?" she asked in a monotone voice, "Give me a date, and I'll let you know if that's soon enough."

Nodding for a moment, he ventured, "May first. Give me until May first. Please."

Tori shook her head, "April first. And I still think that's too long." She gave him a stern look, knowing she still needed him for the repairs. Silently, she cursed him for pushing her. She had learned it was ok to need help in the halfway house, and had struggled with that notion since he had taken that seat next to her on the bus. However, she still found admitting that fact difficult, and she kept her stoic façade firmly in place, unwilling to let him see her inner turmoil.

Staring down at the beautiful pink buds with baby's breath spewing out between them, Tori's heart felt heavy. Giving them the same angry glare she had cast on him, she longed to gingerly reach out and touch one, their scent calling to her from the short distance. Or to smash them; as doing so would have effectively ended her debate.

She wanted to throw her arms around him, and thank him for the gift, but she didn't trust those feelings. She had been given things by a man before, and the pink rose that Eli had presented wrapped in plastic sprang to the front of her mind. She hadn't shared about Eli's rose, the memory of it too painful, and she felt relieved she had kept the secret. Michael wouldn't get her that easily.

In the end, she didn't really accept the flowers, but she

didn't throw them away either. They sat on the table for several days before they were wilted and had to be tossed out. That fact gave Michael hope; enough to keep him going.

They worked hard that day, finishing the floor in the back of the house and were ready to lay the tile in the utility area and the bathroom. Michael had been teaching her how to use the tools and had already shown her how to lay down the grout and position the flooring squares when they did the kitchen and hallway.

She had begun to feel as at ease with those tools as she did with the ones she used to rebuild the motorcycles. The thought made her smile in her quiet way, thinking it would only be a while longer before she could get on with what she really came there to do.

# First Christmas

The work on the house slowed as the holiday approached and getting supplies became more difficult. Being in a small town, shops were not bound by the schedules of a large chain, and therefore would close at odd times to enjoy personal days off for shopping and family time.

They were able to order furniture for their bedrooms, but it would not be delivered until after the New Year. Michael had to convince her to get a bed of her own, talking her into taking a queen sized set to fit her height, along with a small bedroom group. He had insisted she take the larger bedroom as well, to fit the bed of course. He had decided on a simple twin bed and nightstand, with nothing more for his room.

Tori maintained her distance from Michael during their endless hours together the best she could. His pushing her to get the bed bothered her, and she feared he was under the delusion they would one day share it. Resolute on driving him away by the end of March, and meeting their April first deadline, she began telling him every horrific and gruesome story she could think of in hopes of doing so even sooner.

She began by telling him about how she had been brought into the group those last few nights at the bush camp. How the group had raped and beaten her into submission. She expounded upon how she had discovered that alcohol made her life bearable and she had used her body to her advantage when she could. She challenged with all the crimes she had committed, the lives she had taken, and what an undeserving person she really was.

Michael took the news in stride, considering his own shortcomings, the ones he didn't share with others. He tried not to comment on her tales of woe, allowing her to vent her frustrations without judging her. He had done so when they first met years ago, and again more recently when they became reacquainted, but he was beyond that. She was special to him, and her words did nothing to change that fact.

Tori also told him about the abortion in Scottsville, which lay only a few hundred miles from where they lived. She wanted him to see how she qualified as damaged goods, and would never be able to give him all the things that he deserved from a mate.

He considered the story carefully, almost certain the child had belonged to his brother. The thought made him feel odd; especially knowing how his plans were deeply affected. If she were to be his wife, they would never have a family, and it would only be the two of them. In the end, he felt ok with that, as families were for other people, and what drew him to her most was the fact that she *wasn't* like other women, almost as if she had been made especially for him.

The last couple of weeks of the month, they worked on the living room. They had to strip out the old carpet and put in a soft brown replacement. She wanted a bookcase installed, so he helped her build a floor to ceiling job that covered the front wall on both sides of the five foot picture window in the center of it, and adding a narrow bench to form a small nook.

Finally, she picked out a living room group to complete the area: a couch, loveseat, and end tables with large lamps. They were all shades of browns and greens, of course, and made a very homey feel in the small living space they still slept in at night. Fortunately, they had the ensemble in stock and delivered it that same day.

A few days before Christmas, he convinced her to purchase a small tree for their living room, and they placed it in the large picture window, so it could be seen from the road. They used gold and silver ribbon to create bows to decorate it, along with a single strand of pure white lights. It was a very simple thing, not at all extravagant. She insisted she did it for him, but several times he caught her staring at it, lost in thought, and he knew she liked it.

On Christmas Eve, they made their way over to the diner for a small dinner. Trish had decorated the store to the point no space remained untouched, and Michael could feel her tension. Tori had never celebrated holidays, as the Dragons were not what you would have called festive, and he wanted to share stories that would help her understand what they were all about.

He began with a thoughtful smile, "When I was a kid, we always visited family on holidays. Of course, Henry was much older and had already moved away from home by the time I was old enough to remember them, but I had a few cousins and other family members that we visited."

"We would have huge meals, and split up, with the grown-ups sitting at the regular dining room table, while all of us kids sat in the kitchen or ate on a folding table in the garage," he laughed, overcome with enthusiasm as he shared his few happy memories from his childhood.

He explained to her about playing with his cousins and the presents they would receive on Christmas morning. She raised her eyebrow at this, recalling the few presents she had ever received, and the one that had her name engraved on it came to mind.

She stared at her plate as he spoke, allowing herself to briefly wonder what it would be like as a child on Christmas morning before forcing the thoughts away, as they were poison to her resolve. It made no sense to worry about the time that she had lost and could never get back.

Michael shared how Santa worked and that he brought toys to children who had been good during the year. The story made her laugh as he told it, the sound making his heart flutter.

"That's all nonsense," she tried to get him to stop with the playful comment.

He only shrugged in reply, relishing the sound she had briefly allowed to escape her perfectly curved lips. *God, she's beautiful.*

Walking home in the crisp air, Michael wished he could touch her. He would have been content to hold her hand or loop an arm around her as they strolled. Her face flushed when they arrived at the house, he watched her prepare for bed, and realized how far he had fallen for her. *This's really gonna hurt if she drives me away*, he thought to himself. *But I can't worry about that. I still have until April to make my case.*

Laying out their packs as usual, they stretched out, but Michael had no intention of falling asleep. They spoke briefly, but she soon began to breathe in a deep rhythm and he knew his time had come. Silent as a cat on the hunt, he climbed out of his bag and slipped to the back of the house, where he had hidden his surprise safely in his closet the day before.

Bringing out the amp first, he placed it on the floor next to the tree. On the second trip, he brought out the guitar and other items, leaning it up and positioning the case beside it, against the amp. Sliding back onto his bedroll, he stared at it, too excited to sleep. He had never played Santa before, and had an odd sensation as he realized, *this might be more fun than actually getting the presents.*

The next morning, Tori awoke early as usual, and

fumbled around in the dark. Finding her way to the back of house, she donned her workout clothes, and slipped out the front door without noticing anything unusual.

The door only made a small click when she closed it, but it awoke Michael in an instant and his heart began to pound. He wondered if she had seen the gift, and his mind swam with excitement.

Getting dressed, he headed off to join her on her run. He caught up to her two streets over and bade her Merry Christmas as he fell easily into step with her.

She gave him a slight nod, and they arrived back at the house shortly thereafter. Tori fell into her usual sets, doing ten sets of ten of pushups, squats, and whatever came to mind.

Michael kept pace with her, a little more winded than he should have been, and realized he needed to make a habit of it if he were going to keep up with her in the long run. When they finally leaned against the tree to stretch and rest, he ventured to ask if she worked out because she liked to or if she thought she needed to.

"A little of both, I guess," Tori answered after some consideration. "I mean, I started training before I can even remember, and deep down I'm still afraid I might need it again someday, if you know what I mean."

Sadly, he did. Shaking off the dark thoughts, he felt eager to get on with the happiness of the holiday. He could feel the tension mounting as it crept close to time to go back inside.

Allowing her to enter first, Michael hung back at the door to give her a chance to have a look around. His special gift still sat next to the tree, where he had positioned it during the night, and he waited for her to notice it.

When her eyes fell upon it, Tori exhaled a loud shriek, and gazed at him with a wild look in her eyes. Michael deviously grinned from ear to ear as he watched her cover her mouth in surprise, thinking he would never have guessed his quiet and reserved girl would make such a noise.

Bounding over to it quickly, Tori's fingers trembled as she reached out to stroke the headstock and tuning pegs before she lifted it up. It was perfect.

"I want you to write some new songs," he instructed her, "But no more sad ones about your past. I want you to write happy songs, and dream about the future." He smiled at her as he spoke, pretty sure she understood what he meant.

Holding the gift in her hands, Tori knew she should refuse to accept it. As she had done with the flowers, she had no business allowing him to do this; gifts from men were dangerous. But this gift felt so special; it was as if she could hear the instrument calling to her, and she felt powerless to decline, no matter what her fears were telling her.

They set up her new toy there in the living room, and she could not wait to plug everything in and see that it worked. *Oh my God, it's amazing!* She played a series of riffs for him, and gave him a small lesson on how the sound went from the strings, into the pickups, which were made from tiny magnets, and on into the amp through the cord, where the sound came out depending on the settings on all of the knobs.

Michael became thoroughly impressed by all the things she knew and loved the way telling them made her eyes shine. So far, it had been him doing all the teaching between them, with the house and the remodeling. It felt good for her to have the chance to share the things she was proficient at, and he realized finishing the shop should be a strong priority, as it would give them more time for her to take the lead and show her strengths.

The morning began to slip away and the couple had to put the guitar aside to start their Christmas dinner. They had picked up a kit at the supermarket that included everything they needed, with a precooked turkey, dressing, and potatoes. Tori only had to place it into the oven or heat items on the stovetop. An hour later, they were ready to feast upon the first Christmas dinner of her life.

Watching her, he was reminded of their conversation about purchasing a microwave. He smiled, realizing how different she was from most industrialized Americans. She had refused the device because it did not use a flame to cook with, as if it somehow made the food unhealthy. He liked the way she preferred things that were natural, and had been surprised she actually agreed to the heat and serve meal they were about to enjoy.

Michael looked so pleased when they sat down that Tori could not help but smile back at him. Glancing over at her new guitar periodically, she felt a joy beyond words, truly grateful to him for giving her the chance to experience one small part of what she had missed in her abnormal childhood.

Eating the tasty meal comfortably, Michael made sure he complimented her on it periodically.

She knew it hadn't been much to prepare, since everything had been precooked, but still, it made her feel good that he made such a fuss over her. Deep down, she knew he would have to leave in a few months, but for this one day she allowed herself to pretend that was her life and always would be.

Once they had their fill, they moved over to stretch out for a customary, after dinner nap. Taking up seats on their new couch and loveseat, Michael began to snore almost immediately, being particularly exhausted due to his late night exploits. Tori watched him, his hand resting on his muscular chest, the rise and fall in perfect rhythm to the sound.

Lying across the smaller unit, her legs bouncing as they folded over the arm, she thought how different he was. When they had first set out together, she had seen him as a dead ringer for Henry. Studying him, she could see the subtle differences that made him unique.

His hair not nearly as grey, it only had a few strays from the looks of it. His face also looked much younger, having had less years and sun than his older brother. Michael had a different curve to his mouth when he smiled, which she found particularly appealing. Eventually she fell asleep as well, a soft smile planted on her velvet lips.

# Pandora's Box

In the weeks after Christmas, they completed the house, and the couple was finally able to begin on the shop in earnest. They were very pleased with the new overhead door, and made quick work of the rest of the repairs once it had been installed.

Working on the garage became a whole new set of tasks. Michael convinced Tori that she would need a vehicle of her own, and that a truck of some sort would be the best choice. Borrowing Trish's car, they were off on the hunt, finally choosing an older and slightly worse for wear F-150 single cab pick-up. It was a brown color, or at least what remained of the paint was. The interior looked much better after they placed a cover over the bench seat, and basically it served as a work truck.

It only took Michael a few hours to teach her how to drive the stick shift. During that adventure, Tori timidly admitted she didn't actually have a driver's license. "The one I had before was faked. Eddie paid a guy to make it for me."

"Well, if you're lying low, you might want to forgo getting one," he cautioned.

Her expression grew dark as she considered the idea of being found. She had to agree, as it would be one more way of being located, if anyone were looking.

The truck turned out to be a good investment though, as it allowed them more freedom. They took a few days to purchase tools and found a couple of old bikes that would make good projects.

After setting up the shop, Tori began to tear down one of the bikes. A ragged '85 Honda Rebel, she intended to give it to Michael so he would have a way to get around. Being their first project, she took the opportunity to break him in on what all rebuilding entailed.

It being Michael's turn to be the student, she explained to him step by step what she did and why. She laid out all of the parts as she took them off, repairing as she could, cleaning a great deal, and making a list of what she would need to purchase or locate. Taking her time as she worked, Tori began to relax, at home in the house, the garage, and his company.

Michael noticed how dirty her hands got while she worked, but Tori didn't seem to mind. Her fingers moved quickly as she removed the tiny parts and inspected them. Often, she would hum while she toiled, and he liked the way she seemed quite at ease, able to focus so deeply on her main purpose of taking the bikes that were old and broken and making them look like new again.

Of course, they were not in dire need of funds yet, but it would be good to have some income soon enough, and completing bikes would be their source. They had counted the remainder of the money after Christmas, as all of the major purchases had been completed with the final addition of the pick-up. Fortunately, they still had almost $300K, and discussed where they would store it.

Eventually, they decided they would add it in small amounts to their receipts from the sale of the restored bikes until it had all been deposited into the bank, the way normal people keep money. Michael pushed aside his realization that this would be considered laundering if they were caught.

Secretly, Tori hid some of it, unable to convince herself

she would never need a quick getaway fund. She wanted Michael to take some with him when he left, but so far he had refused, only accepting the motorcycle as payment, more or less, for all that he had done for her.

As the only gift he would accept from her, she put extra care into the bike she rebuilt for him. She wanted to express her growing feelings for him the only way she comfortably could, through the love she poured into the machine. She imagined him riding away on it in April, taking this part of her with him to keep, which moved her more deeply than she cared to admit.

January turned out a busy month for the couple in many ways. Their beds were delivered the first week, and they made the transition to sleeping in their individual rooms. Michael did his best to hide his sadness, as sleeping in the small bedroom felt extremely lonely for him after he had become accustomed to stretching out beside her every night.

Lying in his bed while she showered, he allowed himself to imagine the water running over her naked curves; a small consolation of sorts since he lay close enough to hear her activities through the thin wall between the two chambers. He noted that she sang often as well, but took great care never to mention the fact, afraid it would put her on the defensive if she knew of his behavior.

Michael hoped that she slept in the oversized bed they had purchased for her. He peeked into her room on occasion, and it did appear that the covers had been disturbed, a good sign, and he felt pleased she still made progress.

The new year also brought the cold, and afforded them more new experiences for the young woman; things that held joy for both of them. After the Christmas holiday, the town's children had returned to school, but the second week of the month, they had a snow day. Basically, this occurs when two or three inches of snow falls, and locals have a few hours to go out and enjoy it before the sun and the warmth of the ground melts it away.

School canceled for the day, the kids were all out in the swirling flakes, taking advantage of the rare occasion. Tori had never played in snow before, as the Dragons largely kept to the south when winter came, and the few times she had seen it, she had either been not permitted or not interested in exploring it. She stood in the door of the shop watching it fall in wide-eyed wonder.

Michael encouraged her to try it, taking her out to put together a tiny snowman and throw a few snowballs at one another. At first, she did not like the feel of the frost in her fingers, and had wrinkled her nose in protest. However, the smile on his face warmed her, and she soon fell into the moment with him. The couple found themselves laughing heartily while chasing each other around, and he felt overjoyed to see her pleasure at the event.

Quite unexpectedly, the pair became caught up in a rather large snowball chucking contest with a group of boys that seemed to materialize out of nowhere. When it ended, the group disbanded just as quickly; all except for one little guy, who introduced himself as Steven and followed them back to the shop to have a look around.

Christopher, his older brother, found him there a short time later. Pulling him away, the couple could hear him admonishing his younger brother for bothering them, and under duress, the young man had apologized with a shy grin. Michael hadn't thought much of it at the time, but fate seemed insistent that these two young men would be a part of their lives, as their paths crossed constantly after that, especially when they were in the diner.

A short week later, they discovered the pair belonged to Trish, boys she had been raising alone. Their father had left when Steven was still small, preferring to drive a truck over running the diner with his wife. Of course, keeping love alive at a distance is hard to do, and the couple eventually divorced.

After the marriage officially ended, the man found more excuses why he could not make it to town for a visit, then he found days when he could. That being the point where Tori and Michael came in, as the two boys had become like lost souls, which struck a familiar chord with the couple.

Trish's sitter moved away over the Christmas break, and she had been having the boys come to the diner after school. She could have left them at the house alone, but it didn't feel like a good option for her sons, who were only nine and twelve, and needed at least some supervision. They were good boys, and got their homework done, but after that, they had little for them to do at a diner but sit around and be bored, and being there until it closed at 8:00 pm every night wore heavily on them all.

In light of this, things fell together in such a way that seemed to work out to everyone's advantage. Michael had enlisted Trish's help in getting the necessary size to complete his order. She in turn gave a jewelry and lingerie party for some of the women in town, and invited Tori. After convincing the girl to attend, she discovered she wore a size eight ring, which enabled him to complete his special purchase of white gold.

When the time came for him to pick up the set, he simply told Tori he needed to run an errand. He only smiled mysteriously at her inquiries as to what, so she had let him go without making much of it, deducing he was making plans for after he left her come April. She pushed the small ache the thought caused her aside, realizing his leaving would be for the best.

As soon as he rode away on his newly completed machine, Tori made her way down to the diner for a short visit with her new friend, a cup of coffee her excuse. She hated to admit it, but she had grown to cherish Trish and her female companionship, whether she wanted it to happen or not. She arrived at the diner to find the older woman distraught and at her wits' end, so she invited the boys down to see the shop to give their mom a break.

After having a look around at the motorcycles and tools, Tori escorted the young men into her small house. Once inside, she showed them her guitar and how to play it, enjoying the evening and their company.

Michael chuckled in surprise when he returned from picking up his special purchases to find the boys inside learning chords; *this could not possibly be part of her plan to stay aloof.* Taking a seat in a kitchen chair, he thoughtfully watched the three of them as they sat on the couch, a broad grin tickling his lips. The door had been opened, and like Pandora's box, there would be no way to put back what had been unleashed; *she's really making herself at home, whether she can admit it or not.*

Michael had placed the wedding bands in a simple grey pouch made of felt. As he observed the trio, he toyed with it in his pocket, rubbing the rings within. In the weeks that followed, he continued to carry them around with him, stroking them often and waiting for the right time to ask the question that burned in his mind more and more as the days went by.

# The Stuff of Dreams

The days passed quickly, and Michael could feel April coming at him faster than he would have liked. Things had been going fairly smoothly for the couple, so it came as a bit of a surprise when things suddenly took an ominous turn with the beginning of February.

Their bedroom sets had been delivered the month before, and so they each slept alone in a bedroom of the small house. The transition had seemed easy enough, and Michael had been pretty sure Tori slept in her bed, not in a corner. That theory was confirmed when she began to have nightmares.

The first time he heard her cry out in the night, he had leapt out of bed and burst into her quarters. She was indeed sleeping in the bed, or had been, but something in her dreams had frightened her and she stood in the center of the room when he arrived, trying to calm her racing heart.

Seeing the panic in her eyes, he had wanted to comfort her, but she had been angry that he had come in unannounced. He left her alone and went back to bed to think about what could be troubling her, as if her past life were not enough to give anyone bad dreams.

The next day, she had made an excuse and explained that it didn't happen very often. However, three weeks later, it had happened at least half a dozen times that he knew of, and Michael decided he needed to know exactly what she dreamed that frightened her so much. They were working in the shop when he decided the time had come to push the issue, and he gave the effort his best.

"I'm not trying to pry," he explained his intentions, "But it's not going to get any better if you don't let it out. Just talk to me. I promise, I'm not going to judge you. I want to help you."

Leaning over the motorcycle, hands working diligently, Tori tried to come up with another excuse why she should keep the anguish to herself. His pushing her made her defensive, as it should have been clear she didn't want to discuss it. She cut her blue spheres at him, not wanting to face him squarely, expecting him to be angry. The look in his eyes took her breath away, as they appeared hurt and sad, almost in tears.

"I'm not good at talking about things," she admitted in a meek voice with a small shrug, shifting her gaze away.

"I know," she heard him whisper back.

She turned to face him fully, his features grim. *Damn it. Why does he look at me that way? Doesn't he know he isn't supposed to care?* Drawing a deep breath and exhaling it slowly, she allowed their eyes to lock for a full minute as she considered what sharing the dream could mean. *You are letting him get too close, and it's going to hurt like hell when he leaves,* she scolded herself with a clenched jaw.

Laying her tools aside, Tori relented, "Let's go to the diner then. Get an early dinner and have a long talk."

Making their way down the street, Michael stole glances at her, noticing the tension that drew the beautiful lines of her face into an almost angry scowl. He hoped the sharing would ease her suffering, as seeing her that way, the dark puffy skin beneath her lower lashes that meant she wasn't sleeping, tore at him mercilessly.

Taking seats in their usual booth, Michael noticed that Trish's boys were at the café again that evening. It felt odd how their lives had become entwined with the people of the small town, even though Tori had not wanted it to happen, and he smiled to himself thinking about how it had been her that caused it.

Seeing his grin, Tori glanced over to note the boys herself and shook her head. She had no idea what had possessed her the day she first invited them to come over, but like lost puppies, they didn't take long to steal a piece of her heart and a spot in her life. Tori had begun to think she was simply no good at being alone.

Looking at the young men, a sad twinge touched her core as she recalled that she would never have children of her own. Perhaps that's what had motivated her to extend the invitation; like she would always have to make do with borrowing other people's families and lives.

Glancing at Michael, she realized the time he would be moving on lay in the near future, and she hoped he would find a woman to share a real family with after he left her. He deserved the chance, and the realization that he would have it brought her a small amount of peace.

Ordering their dinner of small steaks and vegetables, the two ate in an uneasy silence. Tori felt anxious, not eager to share what disturbed her sleep, the horror of it too real for her to make light of.

However, as soon as the food had disappeared, Michael gently reminded her of the story she had promised him; sharing what the nightmares were all about.

She sat staring at her empty plate and collecting her thoughts. When ready, she took a deep breath and dove in, "I've been having the same type of dreams as long as I can remember; ever since I was a child in the bush camp."

"I'm not sure what has caused them to flare up this badly," she gave a small shrug. "I mean, I've had basically the same dream from time to time, the same *exact* dream. But something about this place, or something else, I don't know, has caused them to come much more frequently and to be much more intense."

"I'm not even sure exactly what the dream is about. It's only a small segment of time, like two or three minutes worth. I'm sitting in a car sometimes, in the back seat, with a man and a woman in front of me, but other times I'm outside of the car, watching it." Tori drew a ragged breath, "There are people screaming and the car burns. Like literally, how a house would burn, and there are flames coming out of it all over. And that's it. When I see it, I'm petrified, and I don't know anything else."

Folding his hands in front of him, Michael studied her pained features. Obviously hard for her to describe, he postulated because she didn't really understand it. He had become accustomed to her quiet and controlled manner, but this was something she could not control, and she hated it.

Looking down at her hands, he noticed the scar that ran across the back of the left one. Without thinking, he reached over and ran his fingers gently across the top of it.

Tori jerked the hand back away from him as if she had been burned and his eyes snapped up to meet hers in surprise. Jaw dropped slightly; he apologized, "I'm so sorry; I don't know what came over me."

She stared at him blankly for several seconds, almost in a state of shock and unable to reply. Drawing several breaths, she recovered but said nothing for a few more seconds. Then whispered, "There's a diner in the dream. Just a glimpse of it; like this one. Before the car burns."

Her breath had become shallow and quick with excitement. "I never remembered that before." Gazing over at the two boys, she felt guilty at befriending them. She had intended to come to that place and live like a hermit. Becoming attached to other people placed them in danger.

"I think the dream is a warning," her voice had become tense, "I should never have made friends here. I should never have allowed you to stay here." She looked back at him; her eyes turned to crystal blue pools, and for a moment she feared he could see her feelings for him in their depths.

Michael shook his head, "It can't be a warning if you dreamt it before you came here. More likely it's a memory, perhaps from before you were taken by the Dragons."

Tori cut in sharply, hitting the table with her hand, "I wasn't taken. They searched all the missing children's records for the last twenty years; I'm not one of them." Her face pained, she continued, "It's like I don't exist, or I came from nowhere."

Michael longed to stroke her hand again, to comfort her somehow. "You do exist and you came from somewhere. I'm afraid the nightmare won't go away until you discover its meaning." He shrugged slightly and went on with a shake of his sandy curls, "And stop worrying about how you've put me in danger. I chose to be here, remember? You need people, Tori. You need to have people to care about and people to care about you. It's what makes you a human being; a person."

She sank back against the booth, dejected. True, the past few weeks she had begun to feel much more relaxed. Chris had brought over some homework to the shop, a bit of math and science, and asked if she or Michael knew anything about it. Tori had wiped her hands on one of her red rags and taken the paper from him to look it over before they moved to the small kitchen table, where she took the time to teach him her way of solving the problems.

"That's not how my teacher showed us to do it," Chris had stated in a patronizing tone.

Tori had only smiled, and explained that often there is more than one way to get from point A to point B. "You just have to decide which way works for you, or makes the most sense to you." She really liked the boy, finding him very smart, and she loved the way he listened and learned what she was willing to teach and share. It brought back fond memories of Henry and her own education, and this pleased her in a sad way.

They worked for a couple of hours on the assignments, and she really wasn't sure if it had been of any use until he brought his test down to show her his 98 a few days later. Tori had never earned grades for herself, but helping him do so well had made her feel ecstatic. Watching him across the diner, she suddenly felt lost, as if she were missing something she should have done.

Turning back to Michael, she switched to German so their words would remain more private should anyone overhear them. "Do you think I have a purpose?" He raised an eyebrow in a questioning manner, but said nothing, so she went on slowly.

"I've been thinking about The Organization. I told the Feds a lot of what I know about them, which isn't much, but I think I could get inside if I wanted to. What if I went after them myself? Tried to put a stop to them on my own. I mean, I have Henry's vault. I could use the equipment and weapons to do something, rather than hide here like a coward, waiting for them to find me." She stared at him intently as she spoke, searching for his approval.

Michael had begun shaking his head back and forth slowly, "You've given up enough. You deserve to have a life. A future. You took out the Dragons, and that's more than your share. You don't need to go all vigilante on those guys. I really don't think they'll bother to come after you." A puff of air escaped him in a disbelieving sound, "I mean, you're just one girl, right? You stay here; you lay low, and you enjoy your new life."

Tori tried to see things from his point of view, but deep down she had a knot in her stomach that wouldn't go away. She was more than just a girl, and she knew it. If the Dragons had kept her a complete secret, what he suggested might have been enough for her, but she knew there were others who had seen her; only once, but it was enough, and it could come back to haunt her and those she cared about.

# Old Friends

Tori had seen lots of bodies in her life. Hell, she was responsible for a large number of them herself. Funny, she had never been to a funeral. The spring morning dawned crisp and clear, and she and Michael dressed in their darkest clothes to join the rest of the town at the small white building a few blocks over. This would only be Tori's third visit to a church, and it reminded her of the time Terry had taken her to meet his friend.

Thinking back, she wondered if Brother Thomas had been the friend, or if it had been the Jesus that the preacher had spoken about that he intended for her to meet. Staring down at the black cover in the book drawer of her dresser as she got ready, she remembered bringing the bible with her from the halfway house.

For a moment, she had thought she wouldn't need it, and started to leave it behind. But some hidden urge had caused her to pick it up anyway, along with the journal, and slip them into her bag next to the German Fairytale book that she had kept hidden in her suitcase.

Sliding the drawer shut, she thought about the reason they were going to the church. On this occasion, they would be honoring the memory of George, the old man who sold them the garage. She found it a little disconcerting that he had succumbed to his illness a short two days after Michael had told her that she should enjoy her life. His passing almost felt like an omen, weighing heavily upon her as they walked together to the small white structure.

Climbing the stairs to the tiny building, Tori could feel the tension in her body, keenly aware of Michael as he moved beside her. She longed to reach over and take his hand, to hold it and know that she was not alone in that moment that terrified her. But she couldn't do that. He wasn't allowed to touch her, and he respected that. She wasn't ready to bring that wall down; not yet.

Choosing a seat close to the back, the couple sat next to one another. Michael allowed her to take the seat on the aisle that ran through the middle of the pews, and he sat to her left. From that vantage point, he appeared to be looking at the speaker, listening carefully to what he or she said about George.

What Michael actually did, was study her. He had tilted himself at an angle that put a small distance between them, yet allowed him to rest his arm on the bench behind her so that his hand would occasionally brush her ebony locks.

Propping his right ankle on top of his left knee, he felt quite comfortable as he watched her changing expression. He could see she tense jawline, perhaps afraid of this tradition she had never experienced. He remembered his mother's funeral, the last one he had attended, and felt an ache for the things we lose over time.

He could see Tori clenching her jaw as the preacher spoke about George's life. How he had worked to provide for his wife and family. He had been a caring man, not one for chasing worldly riches. Glancing across the aisle, Michael could see the pews that held the family.

Tori watched them also; Chris and Steven both crying at the loss of their grandfather. Even Trish, seated next to them, was visibly distraught at having lost her father-in-law. Family meant a lot in that little town, and they had pulled the couple into it, and treated them as one of their own.

His eyes sweeping the interior of the building, Michael could see the front of the small structure had been covered in flowers. They had not gotten to know the old man very well, but from the looks of the mourners, he had been a good man who had left behind many who cared for him.

Reaching up, Michael accidentally stroked the hairs that were closest to his hand. Tori moved slightly, and he felt a jolt of excitement at having gotten away with the small caress. Sitting with her like this, the event could have lasted all day, even if it were a funeral.

The service ended and everyone broke up to go their separate ways. Trish caught the pair out front and insisted they come to the house with the family. Michael had a sudden urge to grab Tori's arm and head for home, not wanting to be a part of the group any longer. Trish hugged the girl, stroking the hairs he had been toying with, and he knew they were going to follow her.

Tori had made a big fuss about keeping to herself, but Trish had seemed to have a sixth sense about the girl and her need to be taken in. The older woman included her whenever she could, always reaching out to the couple and doing whatever she was able to make them feel like a part of the small, close knit community.

Arriving at the massive Victorian, the mood lightened, and although the occasion sad, laughter could be heard as children played, and grownups discussed the future and reminisced about the past. Realizing the situation was all new for her, Michael stayed close to Tori while she looked around with wide eyes and a docile expression.

Eventually, she made her way to the kitchen to join the other women in preparing the meal that had been delivered by the church family. Her exit freed him to visit with the men on the wide veranda in the afternoon breeze, a surprisingly warm day for the tail end of February.

Visually taking in the grounds, he noticed the tall trees that grew around the property. "How old is the house?" he found himself asking. Another elderly man, George's brother Carl, made a long moan as he thought about the answer.

"Well, Marge and Georgie bought this place back in 1960, right after they got married. Before that, it had belonged to another couple, an' I wanna say it was built back before the war."

Michael gathered he meant the Second World War. He smiled at the way the old man spoke, his southern drawl matching that of Trish, but his delivery a great deal slower. The people there were so friendly, so accepting of Tori and himself. They had opened up and brought them in, giving her things she had never had before without question. He felt grateful for that.

Soon, the men were called inside, as the bed had been removed from the dining area, and a large wooden table had reclaimed its position within the house. Michael grinned as he noticed the smaller tables set about for the children along the porch, as more adults had taken over the kitchen table, as well. Taking his place beside Tori, he gave her a small smile, which she returned.

Looking around the spacious kitchen from his vantage point, he could see that it needed many of the repairs and updating that they had recently completed on their small house down at the shop. He could see Tori having a peek around as well, probably thinking the same thing. Their eyes met periodically, and although it would have been rude for them to break into their typical German, their eyes spoke what they were each thinking: this place feels like home.

The delicious meal, a variety of the best dishes from all the neighbors, had been delivered to feed the family. Both Michael and Tori had their fill, each listening to the stories the relatives shared in respectful silence.

Michael knew she had no stories of her own; not like this. Not that she could share with strangers. He could see the somber look in her eyes, painfully aware of all that she had missed, being raised the way that she had been.

After the meal, he gently persuaded her the time had come to go home, and she seemed reluctant to walk away from the warm atmosphere the family created. Ambling quietly along beside him, he could tell she had sunk deep in thought. He knew she would not share them with him, not being her way. She tolerated his presence; he was not her confidant.

When they reached the house, she went to the back and closed the door to her bedroom where he could not see her cry. But she did not cry for herself. She cried for Trish and her sons and the loss they faced. She cried for the families her hand had touched and all the lives she had taken.

Opening the drawer to her dresser, she thought back to her previous visit to a place of worship, remembering Brother Thomas and the words he had spoken to her. He had explained to her about forgiveness; how God had forgiveness in his plan for her. But to receive it she must forgive those who hurt her, and moreover forgive herself.

Laying her trembling fingers on the dark cover of the text, Tori sobbed. In her heart, she wanted the peace that she could see in so many people around her. Slowly lifting the book, it felt heavy in her hand.

Michael had chosen a plain wooden rocking chair for her room, and she sank into it, flipping through the pages of the volume, stopping when she saw the word *Job* at the top of one of them.

Starting at the beginning, she began to read about this man named Job, and all of the bad things God had allowed to happen to him, while rocking gently back and forth in

Michael's chair. Reaching the end, she shifted the tome to close it.

Hugging the bible to her chest, she rested her chin along the top edge, her mind turning as she considered what the story had been about. She thought about the inertia of her own life and how she often felt caught in the flow that carried her forward, whether she wanted it to or not. She could see the resemblance between Job and herself, having everything they cared about taken from them, being at the mercy of greater forces.

Finally, she considered the place that she lived, in the little house with Michael. She could feel her heart skip a beat when she thought about Henry's brother, and she wondered if she could trust the strange feelings she knew were growing inside of her, like the tendrils of a fungus as it spreads across a forest floor.

The world outside remained dark and full of danger. However, in their place, reconciliation; in their place there was forgiveness to be had, if she were strong enough to accept it. Tori began going to the small white church the following Sunday to listen to the preacher talk to her as she sat alone in the last pew. She never mentioned it to Michael, never asked him to go with her. The matter would remain between her and Terry's friend, the one she was finally ready to meet.

# The Life You Have

Tori seemed preoccupied the next few weeks, as if she were thinking deeply about what they had discussed at the diner, as well as the funeral and all it had awakened inside of her. Considering Michael's advice, to enjoy the life she had, she become tempted to give it a try in earnest.

Steven and Chris were coming over daily after school, and Trish had wanted to pay them for taking care of the boys. Michael had insisted it wasn't necessary, having noticed that their visits were helping Tori in ways she did not seem to see for herself.

He watched her when she worked with them, and felt happy that her gentle, nurturing side was finally able to grow and be set free. He knew she had begun sneaking off to the church on Sundays, but as she kept the activity a secret, he allowed her that time for herself, and could see the changes slowly taking place within her.

Working on the motorcycles, Tori talked to him more than ever. She would explain everything, and he did his best to be a good student; she had learned far faster than he did, when their roles had been reversed. As she directed him, he could feel her watching him, and wondered what she was thinking.

Michael kept the bag with his surprise for her inside his pocket. He would often reach his hand in to rub the two rings through the soft grey felt. He had insisted on coming to

Texas with her out of loyalty, because it had been the right thing to do. He had promised Henry and Terry both he would take care of her, and he had done that. But, he had remained there because he loved her, and he could think of no place on earth he would rather have been.

Michael lived in purgatory, strung out on the longing to give her his special gift. He grew quieter as she opened up to him, afraid of what he might say or do and the consequences his actions could hold. He wasn't ready to make his move, not sure if her increasing comfort meant she had grown to love him in the way that he loved her. He feared she was happy because she would soon be rid of him for good. And of course, his change in behavior had an effect he could not have predicted.

Tori began to regret her choice to make him leave, and she struggled to understand his quieter persona. She speculated that he was cutting ties with her, and the realization made her forlorn. One minute she would be thinking how good it would feel if he were to stay. Then the next, she would consider how sending him away would be the best option for both of them. She pondered the question endlessly and could not decide which emotions were the truth.

Terry's words came back to haunt her, and she would shake her head in disgust when she recalled them. *"There will always be people,"* he had said. She did not want to let people get close to her. Having them around meant so much more to her; so much more to risk for who she was. She did not want to care for anyone, including Henry's brother, but she did, and she hated Terry for being right in the end.

By the last week of March, the weather grew warm, and summer would soon be at hand. Michael was finally becoming adept at working on the motorcycles, and Tori felt pleased with his efforts. To test his skills, she gave him a list of tasks to complete, and then sat back to watch him perform them. A smile crossed her lips as she realized how far he had come, and she pondered how he would use his new skills after he left her.

The thought brought her mood down, so she excused herself to retrieve a bottle of water from the house. Considering what finally being alone in her life would mean, she found herself staring at the empty table in their tiny kitchen; the table that had once held a large bouquet of pink roses she had never allowed herself to accept. With a deep sigh of regret, she grabbed two bottles of water from the fridge, one for herself and one for the man who plagued her.

The girl returned to discover that Michael had removed his shirt to combat the heat of the afternoon and the sight of him caused her mind to race in a wild and unnerving direction. She could feel her face flush as she watched his muscles move beneath the smooth flesh of his broad shoulders. He had a thin mat of curling hairs on his chest, and for an instant she thought of running her fingers through it.

With only a few days before his departure, she discovered that old familiar ache burned inside her; the craving to touch and be touched. She struggled to push the longing away, and she sought desperately to hide her shameful thoughts and desires. She knew such feelings were not to be trusted after the pain they had brought her in the past.

Deep down, this made Tori feel beaten. She felt fairly certain he would never want her in that way. He had told her once about his past loves, and she had known from their first meeting he thought of her as a dirty whore. *All the more reason to guard your heart,* she warned herself with a sigh.

He hardly looked at her as she handed him the refreshing offering. Opening the bottle, he chugged it quickly and got back to work without giving her a second glance. *See? You brought this on yourself*, she thought wryly, *keeping him away when you had the chance to be close to him. He doesn't want you now, if he ever did.* With a heavy breath, she resigned herself to watch in silence, sticking to the course she had chosen.

That night, Michael lay in his bed and kept to his routine, listening to her through the wall. Removing the rings from their grey felt bag, he read the inscription inside of the smaller shiny band of metal. He knew the first was coming, and that the time had come to push the issue of their relationship. He had seen the way she stared at his half naked body when she brought his water to him, and only hoped he could take it as a sign that she had grown ready.

The following morning, they were adding the final touches to their latest rebuild, when Michael guided them into an unexpected conversation.

Tori, taken by surprise at his sudden talkative streak, found it odd and a bit disconcerting. Playing along, she made small talk with him for a bit. Eventually, he steered the discussion towards his plans for the future, and she nervously continued down the terrifying path.

Michael squatted while working on the task at hand, and pretending to complete the bike. "I don't want you to be offended that I'm not chasing you around the house or anything. If I were that kind of guy, I assure you I would be." *Easy,* he breathed to himself, *take it slow, or you'll scare her off.* He wanted to test her, but he would have to take his time about it.

Tori leaned on one of the workbenches, and twisted around so she could look at him and hear him more clearly. In light of her recent thoughts, his words astounded her, and she almost blurted out that she wanted him to stay. Drawing a deep breath, she willed herself to remain calm.

Michael had been watching her, once again admiring her rear end as it stuck out behind her. Deciding for more, he smiled, turning away from her as he spoke. "I made myself a promise long ago, the next woman I'm with will be my wife." His chest heaved, having laid his plan at her feet, and desperately hoping she wouldn't stomp on it. He still pretended to work on the motorcycle in front of him, loosening and tightening the same bolt repeatedly, unable to force his mind on to the next step.

Tori could feel her heart pounding in her chest, and her face no longer smiled. She took several minutes before she replied, seeming to be choosing her words carefully. This time even she noticed the weight of the silence. "So… are we still friends?" she posed the question timidly. It had been many weeks since they had spoken so openly, and she grew apprehensive of where it might lead.

"Of course we are," he answered in a strong voice, "We're best friends. I hope you'll at least let me visit or keep in touch after I've moved on." Rocking his jaw from side to side, he avoided meeting her gaze.

She made no reply, so he stood from where he had been busying his hands to steal a glance in her direction. She hadn't moved from the counter, and rolled her eyes as she looked away, shuffling uncomfortably.

"So, you're still planning on leaving then?" she queried, her voice barely above a whisper.

Michael kept his tone even while shuffling towards her, "I thought that's what you wanted. No strings. No ties."

Tori shrugged, bobbing her head lightly while staring at the wall in front of her, "I may have changed my mind a little on that. I mean, you've proven to be quite useful at times." She did not smile as she looked at him with guarded desire in her eyes.

He let her stew for a moment before letting her off the

hook, keeping his own voice low, "I'm not going anywhere any time soon, if you permit me to stay."

A smile spread across her lips like a sunrise that cracks the crest of a mountain. Michael became lost in her blue eyes and thought of the bag of rings in his pocket. *Not yet*, he warned himself, *she agreed to let you stay; give her time to adjust before you push for the next step.* They spent the rest of the day in comfortable relief, as if the weight of the future had been lifted with the removal of the deadline.

The following morning, Tori wasn't in her room when Michael awoke. He surmised she hadn't returned from her run, and made his way out to the kitchen. He liked the way she took care of herself, and had begun to join her more regularly. He had done his share of PT over the years, but had no great love of it. This girl seemed obsessed with it.

Looking around the front part of their house, he thought about all the time they had spent working to restore it. He liked the way she chose simple things, such as the plain brown sofa and the tiny table in the kitchen. He realized it could be because of the way she had been raised, outdoors, living in hammocks and cabins, then the open road for all those years. They wouldn't be much for most women, but for Tori, they were far more than she had ever had or dreamed of.

Spying her stretching under her tree, he grabbed a bottle of water for her and took it outside. "Good morning," he called in a cheerful voice. She did not reply, but gave him a slight smile when he handed her the container. "So, what's the plan today?" He felt eager to be close to her, now that there would be a chance for their future and he did not have to guard himself so closely.

She looked deep in thought for a moment, and then said wistfully, "I don't really know. I need to shower and make breakfast, and then I think we can decide." They had a buyer for the bike they had finished, and would be ready to start the next one if they wanted. Somehow, spending the day doing other things seemed more appealing, and she thought of playing some of her new music for him to critique.

Michael only half listened to her at that point, having seen the glimpse of chrome down the street at the café that faced their shop. Her back turned as she looked at him, he felt pretty sure she had not noticed it.

"Yeah, that sounds good," he shift his gaze back to her. "I have some things I need to take care of, though. Why don't you start without me, and I'll catch up when I get back." She gave him a sly smile, and went on inside without questioning him.

Michael followed her into the house to pull on his jacket. Hearing the water in the bathroom for her shower, the image of her standing naked beneath the spray muddied his thoughts, but he shook his head to clear it, knowing he had to check out what he had seen as soon as possible. Locking the door behind him, he strolled down the road towards the diner at a brisk pace. When he entered, he knew right away who owned the bike.

The dark haired man in leather and boots sat at the counter, talking with Trish in a playful manner. "Buenos dias," Michael said as he took the seat next to him, watching the stranger with a slanting cut of his eyes.

"Buenos dias," came the reply, and he could see the visitor sizing him up. He ordered coffee, and then sat sipping it, the two men side by side for several minutes in silence.

Of course, Michael and Enrique had never met, but she had spoken of him, and he felt confident this was the man from her description. Eventually, he continued in Spanish, eyeing Trish carefully as he inquired, "You who I think you are?"

The stranger nodded as he drank from his cup, replying

coolly, "Yeah, I thinks I am." He cut his eyes at Michael for a moment, and they both stood to move to a booth so they could talk more privately and keep an eye down the road.

Michael took Tori's usual seat, so he could watch their home out the window to his left. Enrique was content to sit staring at him, still playing his cards tight while he drank from his steaming mug.

"How did you find us?" Michael posed the question bluntly, thinking they had covered their tracks pretty well, buses and hiking and all. They had been there for months, and they thought they were safe.

Enrique did not give too much away; "I had help," he admitted mysteriously. He continued in a listless tone, "I guess you're with her now."

Michael nodded, "More or less. I'm looking after her, giving her some stability in her life."

Enrique nodded. He knew what he had meant, having seen the chaos that ruled her first hand. They had been in Florida the first time he had laid eyes on her, when the Dragons had brought her up from Brazil. Eddie and the guys were eager to show her off to the Scorpions and their leader, Brett Spears.

# Eddie's Prize

New to the group, Enrique had only been with the Scorpions a year. He had heard about this other crew, the Dragons; one of the several that circulated, working for The Organization. Brett and the Farrell boys went way back, twenty-five years or so.

They had some kind of wager going, about secret weapons and some other bullshit. Enrique had never really understood it, or taken it seriously. The night they had rolled into their camp with her, Brett had been fit to be tied.

When Tori climbed off the bike, the Scorpions gathered around to give her a once over. She looked pretty skittish back then, hadn't really settled into her role as a Dragon yet. She was big, standing about six foot tall; real easy on the eyes, too.

Brett had looked her up and down, and then asked his old friend if he minded giving up a taste. Eddie had grinned broadly, telling him to have his fill, and anyone else who was interested, dropping a tube of gel on the table for them to use. The girl had stared at it, what it meant painfully obvious. Each group held twelve men, and it would be a long night.

At dusk, Brett had walked over to the girl, running his hand along her jaw and turning her face to look her in the eye. She didn't put up any resistance when he touched her, allowing him to remove her jacket and kiss her deeply while his hands explored her from the curve of her breasts to her smooth round backside. Eventually, she stepped away from him to remove the rest of her clothes while he and the rest of the group watched.

The girl was tall, with thick dark hair, almost black, that hung to the crack of her rear end in shiny waves. Enrique, a lower member, would have to wait his turn to touch her. Brett would be first, if he wanted it, and from the look on his face, Enrique could see that he wanted it. Of course, he could have waited and chosen to be last; as the leader of the group, he always had seniority and the most choice.

She didn't put on much of a show as she stripped, but with a body like that she really didn't have to. She had a slender build, toned, a flat muscular belly and nice round breasts; all natural, too. When she turned to take ahold of Brett, Enrique could see the scar on her left breast. Brett had seen it too, and ran his finger lightly over the bite mark while she grabbed him by the front of his jeans and began to unhook his belt. He knew what the mark meant; she was Eddie's most prized possession.

Tori handled him rough, pushing him back against the table and working herself against him. She tugged at his pants until she could reach him. He had been soft when she pushed her hand down, but it didn't take long for him to respond to her. Holding his head and neck with her left hand, she appeared to be in charge of the situation, her hand gripping his hair as she chewed on his tongue, but it didn't last long.

Seizing her arm and pulling himself free, Brett twisted it behind her and forced her chest down onto the table. Popping the tube open, he gave her a squirt with his right hand and massaged it a little, his left still holding her arm pressed to her back as she lay in playful submission. Freeing himself from the confines of his jeans, he pushed his way into her with little effort, still holding her arm in the twisted position.

Brett made quite a show of fucking her, but he didn't take much time to finish. When he was satisfied, she didn't bother to move from where he had placed her, as the next few took their turns. Watching, Enrique got the feeling she was drunk, maybe on the verge of passing out. His breath had become short with anticipation, knowing he would take his time with the dark haired beauty.

Finally, his chance came. Stepping up to her, he ran the backs of his fingers down her spine, watching her twitch. Taking her by the arm, he hoisted her up for a moment so that she stood beside him. Nuzzling her cheek with his nose, he kissed her. She kissed him back, but sloppy, and he knew he had been right about her being wasted.

Laying her back down, he popped his pants open and dropped them enough to work himself out. Making sure she was slick enough, he made it inside with only a slight effort and began to work her in deep heavy strokes, enjoying the way she moaned.

Reaching over his head, he pulled his shirt off with one hand so he could feel her naked skin rub against his chest while he lay over her, forcing their bodies together.

Lacing the fingers of his right hand with hers, he began to drive her hard enough to make her cry out as she gripped the edge of the table with her left. His own left hand slid easily over her, caressing the side of her breast, down to her bare hip, enjoying the curve of her body beneath him.

He worked himself to the point of finishing, and then he pushed himself in completely and held still, willing himself to hold out. She panted loudly, taking the full thickness and depth of him, still gripping the edge of the table as he remained motionless inside her.

The urge passed, and he squeezed the flesh that covered her left ribs as he worked himself up again, nibbling her ear while he slammed against her bare skin with a deep driving motion. Finally, he began to pulse inside her, and then lay still for a moment gasping for air.

She squeezed his hand for a brief moment, and he ran the back of his left hand down her spine once more before he released her and stepped away, smiling to himself at how she had enjoyed the dirty way he fucked her.

Enrique kept a close eye on the girl after their first encounter, already considering how he might acquire the young woman. Tori woke up on the ground next to the table at sunrise, wrapped in a sleeping bag. She made a face as she cleaned herself before she dressed, frowning at the flesh that covered her ribs on the left side. She closely inspected the fresh bruises he had left there in his excitement, causing him to wonder if she recalled how she had received them. Once she was dressed, she located a bottle of water and began rehydrating while she collected herself.

The Dragons and Scorpions were scattered all over the place, spread out sleeping or starting their day. Seeing her sober, Enrique did his best to establish himself in her realm of being, walking up to her and placing his hands on the sides of her neck, so his palms grazed her cheeks. She did not resist when he leaned forward to put his mouth over hers.

Enrique liked kissing her, and she wasn't shy about their swapping spit, so he did this to her periodically, until Eddie pulled him aside for a lesson on when and when not to touch another man's bitch. Tori seemed to have picked up on the vibe, and took great pains to avoid him and the rest of the Scorpions after Eddie's reprimand, unless she had been instructed to take care of them.

The days went by with a myriad of activities, the guys talking about bikes and jobs and business. The Organization had a full list of directives, and clearly, both groups would be busy for a while. Each night, the Dragons shared her with the Scorpions, as Eddie was quite proud of his new toy, and each night Enrique fucked her in his slow, grasping manner. He loved the way she responded to him, and fully believed that she equally enjoyed their encounters.

The fourth and final night, things took a morbid turn, and the group got a chance to see firsthand why the girl seemed to have a deep appreciation for Vodka. At first, Eddie tied her wrists with a short piece of rope. He used a second, longer piece and tied her hands over her head, so that she hung from one of the supports to the metal roof that covered the table.

She never cried out, and endured their torture, but it became clear the twins wanted to show off how much she could take as she dangled limply between them. Afterwards, Enrique understood why she drank. He chose not to touch her that night, as all of the others passed, as well.

Cutting her down when they were finished, the pair left her in a heap on the ground and Tony, a member of the Dragons, covered her with a blanket for the night, the welts standing out against her creamy skin, and the blood and goo oozing from her assaulted regions.

The last day, Brett had seen enough. The two groups were gathered as the Dragons were preparing to move out, having places to be and work to do. Relaxing over their final conversation, Eddie took Brett's comments in stride, "Don't get me wrong, she serves a purpose, but girls don't need fifteen years or so of training to learn to fuck, man." He had smirked at his old friend, trying not to be too harsh on him.

Eddie only nodded his agreement. Tori had been watching him intently, as she never missed what went on around her when sober. Eddie glanced over at her and gave her an evil grin.

Giving her a nod, he made a signal with his right hand and bobbed his head towards one of the Scorpions. Instantly, she leapt up from where she had been squatted and attacked the man.

Her movements were swift and sure, no one in the gathering expecting it, least of all her victim. Rolling on the ground, he went into defensive mode, but she already had the advantage and had bloodied his mouth and nose before knocking him onto his back and shoving her knee into his chest, the weight of her holding him in position.

The blade of her knife shone bright when she threw her right arm up and released the steel with a loud pop of the trigger; Enrique sat in shocked horror staring, unable to look away from what was coming. However, Eddie had stepped forward and caught her wrist, preventing her from bringing the knife down.

"Easy, love," he soothed her, "We are after all... friends here." He had a smug sneer on his face as she jerked her arm free from him, glaring down at her prey in disgust at having been prohibited from finishing.

Rising slowly, Tori snapped the blade closed, and took a few steps back. She allowed the wounded man to roll over onto all fours before standing, shifting her eyes over to Eddie to await further direction. Enrique continued to stare at her heaving chest, in awe of the young woman and the havoc she was capable of bringing down upon her target.

With a wave of his hand, her owner called her off, and she visibly relaxed, returning to her former position and taking deep breaths to cleanse herself. The remainder of the Scorpions sat in stunned silence, not sure if what they had witnessed had been real.

Eddie stretched out next to Brett once more, chewing on a stick and smiling at his accomplishment. No one ever said anything else about the girl, or made reference to what she was. They all knew Eddie had completed the construction of his secret weapon, and Brett paid up on their wager.

Enrique became addicted to the girl after that first taste.

The Scorpions and the Dragons did not work closely with one another, but they met up from time to time for various occasions. Eddie didn't always share his woman with the Scorpions, but when he did, Enrique always had his fill.

He liked the way she felt beneath him, the way she willingly accepted whatever was being given. That is until the two groups had a falling out. Brett had a thing for the girl as well, and during the last time the two groups had hung for a few days, he made Eddie an offer. He wanted to buy the girl and felt $300K a fair price. Enrique thought he was crazy; an insane sum to pay for a woman.

Eddie had angrily informed him she wasn't for sale, no matter the price. A heated discussion had ensued, and they almost came to blows. In the end, the Dragons dropped off the grid after they went their separate ways, presumably so that Eddie could use his secret weapon to make his next move.

# By Chance

Sitting in the diner with Michael, the pair drank their coffee in silence, each lost in their own thoughts. Trying to figure out how to gain the upper hand, Enrique needed to rethink his plan. Going through what he knew, he recalled what had happened after the two groups had gone their separate ways, and how he had gotten onto Brett's bad side.

The Scorpions, loyal to The Organization, were on assignment in Arizona when he got pinched. Enrique found it odd that he got a visit from a federal agent almost as soon as he was in custody.

The agent, a shorter man with a slight build, had not identified himself, stipulating that he had an offer that would ensure his freedom if he cooperated; an offer Enrique could not refuse.

A week later, he was placed in a halfway house in LA, where he was to stay for a month before returning to the Scorpions to gather information for the Feds. They had given him a small flip phone and told him to keep in touch. Enrique used the phone to contact the Scorpions, who did not seem too eager to have him return to their group.

Thinking back, Enrique remembered how his plan had spun into chaos when Tori Farrell turned out to be at the same halfway house, trying to rebuild her life. *It wasn't real smart for me to offer her up to Brett like that,* he thought to himself presently. He had tried to use her to save his own skin and buy his way back into the group; a decision he had later regretted.

Allowing Trish to refill his cup, Enrique remembered he didn't think things could get any worse once he was on the run and trying to keep the Scorpions or anyone else from finding the thing that meant the most to him: Tori. But somehow, the odd phone call he had received a few weeks ago in Ohio had proven he had been wrong about that.

When he answered the call, a male voice on the other end had known his location down to the address, and instructed him to exit the building and meet him at the café a few blocks away. Flipping the device shut, he had considered not going, but since the caller had warned him people he cared about would pay the price if he didn't, he decided it couldn't hurt to go see who it had been and what they wanted.

Enrique had a bad feeling when he saw the same federal agent with coal black hair waiting in a corner booth for him as he entered the diner. Taking a seat across from the short man, he had tried to look calm, but on the inside he could feel his heart pounding.

"Well," he huffed loudly, "Didn't expects you. How'd you find me?"

The agent declined to elaborate, stating, "We're short on time and need to get to the point." His words and tone were completely controlled.

"Ok, so what's the point?" Enrique challenged with a wave of his upturned hand.

"The point is, we had a deal. A deal which you have not upheld." The agent did not mince words as he stabbed the table with his finger. "You were supposed to return to the Scorpions and should be with them, gathering information for us."

Enrique, rubbing his chin for a moment, laid back with his elbow on the rear side of his seat and tried to explain.

"See, what happened was, there was this girl in the house with me, and she got me into some trouble… and I had to leave. I haven't been able to catch up to the Scorpions, so…"

The agent held up his hand, cutting him off, "Yes, we know about Tori Farrell. We also know the two of you were quite chummy." Enrique's brown eyes grew wide with surprise, while the man continued, "What we've decided, is to give you a second chance. We want you to help us with the girl."

"The girl," Enrique scoffed, "What the hells do you want with her? I thought you guys was helping her get clean and alls that shit."

The agent shrugged, "Things change. You see, she's a special girl. She knows things. And she has a job to do; kind of like you, only she isn't doing it. We want you to go and remind her of what it is she needs to be doing." He paused to give Enrique a chance to think about what he had said, and then went on, "And there's another problem we need you to take care of."

"See, she's very cunning." He cracked a half grin, "She manipulates men like they were play-dough. She has a man there with her, one that we're certain she's currently involved with, if you get what I mean."

Enrique felt a stab of jealousy, as he did, in fact, know what he meant.

"You'll need to eliminate him from the picture; how, we don't care." He waved a hand as a suggestion for solving the problem. He extended the pause to ensure Enrique had understood his new assignment, then continued, "What you want to do after that, is convince her she needs to finish her job. The special job that Eddie Farrell and the Dragons trained her for."

Enrique interrupted, "And what job is that?"

The agent smiled at him, nodding slightly. "She knows.

She's in a little town in Texas, down south. I have it marked for you." He slid a map across the table as he spoke. "Just go pick her up, convince her you two make a great couple, and get her back on task."

Enrique poked at the map with a shrug, "I'm not doin' anything until I knows what the job is. And what do I get outta alls this anyways?"

The stranger continued to smile, "She'll have to tell you about the job, and if, by chance, you both survive," he paused for a moment, giving him a shrug, "You get to keep the girl."

Enrique started to laugh loudly, "You can't just give her to me. It's not like you *own* her."

The agent's smile shifted, looking more like a sneer. "Well," he agreed, his blue eyes shining, "Technically you're right, we don't own her. But, we are the Feds after all; we can do," he paused to open his palm towards the ceiling, "Whatever we want with people. If you don't believe me, just ask her when you see her. Ask *her* what we're able to do with people."

Enrique swallowed, considering the way he had emphasized the word *her*. Standing, the agent exited the shop, leaving the other man staring at the map.

Shifting in his seat, he glanced around and reached for the folded parchment. Opening it up, he found the town circled with a blue ballpoint pen. Leaning back, he pushed out a breath through pursed lips, thinking about what he should do. The last time they were together, he had realized he loved her, and those feelings hadn't changed.

Of course, the promise of having her felt great, since he had wanted her for a long time. The only problem, he had left her in tears in LA. He knew she might not be so receptive to him showing up, especially if she suspected that he had been sent by the Feds or that he had offed her current lover to get to her.

Tucking the map inside his jacket pocket, Enrique stood and headed out the door. He knew he would have to have a really good story as to how he had located her. Hell, he might just pretend it was an accident. He could feel himself swelling as he thought about the last time he had seen her.

Tori had been lying over the wooden chair in the office of the little bar where they were hanging out. She had been naked, too, as he had just fucked her in that dirty way she loved, and he had stared down at her creamy white curves as he stood over her. Smiling to himself as he started the bike, he couldn't wait to get to Texas.

# Dangerous Ground

Pulling himself back to the diner, Enrique focused on the man who sat across the table. "Make sure you look her in the eye when you're with her," he commanded. "She deserves that."

Michael shifted uncomfortably as he peered out the window towards the shop, realizing what he had meant. Nodding, he replied, "Yeah, I got that covered. Maybe I have more respect for her than you."

Enrique grinned at his comment, remembering the bar in LA and the way she had let him take her there, even when she wasn't drunk. She liked it nasty; he was sure of it. But he resisted the urge to remark how much they had both enjoyed it. Shifting in his seat, he changed the subject, as they had business to discuss. "So, you two gonna stays here?"

"What's it to you?" Michael challenged, his heart rate increasing at the prospect of trouble.

"Easy man," Enrique gave him a small wave of his hand, "Just lookin' out for her. She's… special." He had come there with the intention of reclaiming her, but since it had been Michael who had come to meet him, he realized that would not be an easy task.

Michael nodded heavily, "Yeah, she is. And yes, we intend to settle down, build a life together." He felt his embellishment justifiable.

Enrique shifted nervously at the news, and inquired,

"Well, maybe I could go down and sees her; I wouldn't stay long."

Michael shook his head slowly, "Naw, man; she's doin' really well now. The last thing she needs is a visit from the past to shake her all up again."

Enrique smiled, thinking that might be what she *did* need. He could see that this man loved her, and wanted to make things right for her. Drawing a deep breath while licking his lips, he considered his options.

He had been haunted by her memory ever since he had left her. And not because he adored fucking her either; she was talented in other ways, as well. If Eddie hadn't scarred her up so bad, she would've been a real beauty, like she had been when he first saw her all those years ago. Not to mention all the things she knew and could do; indeed a real prize.

However, he wanted more than to simply own her, and that fact scared him, if he were honest about it. He had told many a girl that he loved them to get his way. With Tori, they weren't just words, and he had come to realize, he actually meant it. *Feelings like those are dangerous; they cause men to do stupid shit and make bad choices.*

Besides, she had been with the Dragons since she was a little girl. She probably had no memory of any other life. If this man was willing to give her one, it would be cruel of him to pull her away from it. *I love her;* he debated with himself, *but do I love her enough to give her away; leave her with a man who can give her a better life?*

Releasing a deep sigh, he turned in his seat so he could view the garage, as well. The front door had been pulled up, and he could see her moving around inside the shop. She rolled the wheel to a motorcycle around from the side, her long dark hair a sharp contrast to her white tee as she stooped over.

151

"She really should've been someone else." He said the words aloud, not really talking to anyone, "A model or something."

The other man nodded his agreement, knowing her life was not the one she was meant to have.

Enrique looked back at Michael, feeling defeated. "I gave her my number." Reaching inside his jacket to show off his little flip cell, "You guys ever get any trouble, you make sure she calls me," he tapped the device.

Michael shrugged, thinking to himself, *we'll never be that desperate*. "Make sure she doesn't see you," he instructed as the other man stood to leave.

Enrique dropped a $10 bill on the table and walked out the door.

Michael sat for several minutes, listening to the bike start up and head out of town in the opposite direction of their shop. Taking a few more gulps of his coffee, he watched as Tori continued to work on her newest project. His mind turning, he realized they were on dangerous ground. If Enrique had found them, others would follow; it was only a matter of time.

Raising his chin and running his right hand across his jaw, he knew he would have to make his move soon. They were going to need a strong relationship if they were going to depend on each other fully when the time came, one way or the other.

Pulling the felt bag out of his pocket to rub, he thought about how he wanted to approach the subject without spooking her or making her suspicious. He didn't know all the details about Enrique or anything else, and asking at the moment would only complicate things.

*First things first*, he told himself as he stood to leave. Giving Trish a wave, he headed out the door and trudged back to the shop. Making it to the gentle slope of the entrance, he walked all the way up behind her before he realized he had invaded her space, where she bent over inspecting the bike.

Noticing him, she stood up straight, spinning sharply to look him in the eye; shocked by his behavior. Instantly hit with cold feet, he took half a step back, running his fingers through his sandy brown locks.

Seeing this, she broke into a wide smile. If they had been closer, she might have kissed him, being far too attractive at the moment to resist without great effort. "What's the matter," she cooed in a soft voice. "You look a little haggard."

Nodding, he agreed, his hand combing his hair again. "I have something on my mind," he began awkwardly, "It's been bothering me for weeks, actually," he confessed. Shifting his weight from one leg to the other, he took the plunge, "Would you marry me?"

Tori looked stricken. There was nothing he could have said that would have shocked her more. Taking a deep breath, she tried to back away, finding herself planted against the motorcycle behind her. He didn't move towards her, and just stood staring, waiting for her response. "You can't be serious," she stammered, her mind in chaos. *Where in the hell did this come from? Has he gone insane?*

He nodded as if she had spoken the words out loud; giving her a small laugh, "Pretty crazy, huh? I just can't help it. I'm stuck here, at this point, and I can't do anything else until I deal with this." He watched her intently as he continued. "You can say no. I'd be ok with that. I just feel it's time to move forward with our relationship."

Tori stared at him, slack-jawed as she agreed, "Yeah, me too. I thought maybe we would date or something though." She shrugged absently, lips curling slightly, still in shock.

Her words encouraged him a little, and he managed a

smile, shaking his head. "I thought that's what we'd been doing since we got here," he teased her, trying to break the tension, glad to see she returned his grin.

Nodding, she put him to the test. She had folded her hands in front of her, palms pressed together, and pointed at him with both index fingers as she lightly tossed out, "So, ok then. If you have a ring, I'll marry you." She said the words flippantly, expecting him back down.

Grinning sheepishly and looking at the ground, he reached into his pocket for the grey bag, saying quietly, "I don't have a ring."

Tori almost felt disappointed as a look of relief crossed her face.

"I have two," he continued, lifting his face to look her in the eye as he loosened the pouch and allowed the shiny circles to slide out onto his opened palm.

Tori stared at the pair of rings in wide-eyed awe. They were plain white gold, a silvery color that reflected the light like the chrome on the bikes she loved to restore. They were beautiful, and they were perfect.

Shifting her gaze up to his face, she could see him patiently waiting for her to give a real response. Slowly closing her mouth, she stared into his eyes for a full minute, allowing herself to take it all in.

Michael could hear the blood swooshing in his ears, not believing he had come out and asked her. After all his careful planning and patience, he let one visit from an old flame push him into trying to force her to commit to him.

Beginning to think he had blown it all, she reached up and closed his fingers around the objects, holding his fist in both hands for a moment.

"What day is this?" her voice quiet, she held his gaze.

Confused, he thought for a moment, and then stammered "April first." *Fuck me, now she thinks this is a joke.* "This isn't a prank," he gushed, "I'm serious about this. See? Yours is engraved. See, look at this," he had freed his hand and held the ring out to her.

Her hands trembling, she took it from him and peered at the inside of the circle. *For Tori, love of my life.*

Tears spilled over from her crystal blue eyes. She looked back and forth, from the ring to his deep brown orbs, remembering the last man who had claimed to love her. *But this is different.* Michael hadn't asked for anything before this. Hadn't made any demands, other than expressed the desire to be close to her, to be allowed to remain with her. Suddenly she connected the date – *this is the day he was supposed to leave.*

She had set the date arbitrarily, months ago. That was before he had chiseled his way inside her heart and mind; before she knew him as a person, and not only as Henry's little brother. "So you wanna give me a ring, huh?" she asked quietly, her tone almost mocking as she studied the inscription.

"No," he answered almost too quickly and her eyes snapped to his, glaring at him in surprise. "I wanna give you something far more valuable to me than that."

He had spoken with conviction. The pause became pregnant with anticipation before he elaborated, "I wanna give you my name."

Staring at him, her eyes didn't waver. Her breath a slow, deep pant, she nodded her head deliberately, "Ok, then we need to set a date."

Relieved, Michael couldn't hold back any longer. Reaching forward, he looped his arm around her waist and pulled her tight against him. Arms locked around her, he hugged her in a strong embrace, rocking her side to side in a gentle swaying motion. "I was thinking today," he whispered quietly into her long dark hair.

# Who I Am

Tori only took a few moments to realize she wasn't going to argue and began closing up the shop. Michael set off to the house and secured it as well, before they headed down the street to the courthouse. Holding hands while they walked at an excited pace, he remembered the day they met Marge and George to purchase the garage. It had been a stressful day but had ended a happy occasion. He hoped today's venture turned out as well.

Making their way inside, they found the county clerk's office and made their request. They each had to sign the forms and provide their identification. Tori seemed nervous as the clerk looked over her tiny emancipation card.

After a moment, the woman told them they would have to wait, as she would have to get clarification about the situation. Tori looked angry as they made their way over to the seating area to await the decision.

Sitting next to her, Michael rubbed her shoulder, trying to calm her. "I'm sure its ok. Probably a formality."

Cutting her eyes at him, she spewed in a bitter tone, "I bet it isn't." Clenching her hands into fists a few times, she tried to calm herself.

Finally, Michael suggested soothingly, "Explain what's going on; get it out of your system. Stewing about it isn't gonna help."

"What's going on is the FBI is fucking with me, and they

have been since they found me." She practically hissed the words, "That Dr. Bennet, who was on my committee, is a lying son of a bitch, and I have no way to prove otherwise." She looked at Michael, her expression pleading for help.

Catching a stray hair to smooth for her, he encouraged her, "Go on."

Drawing a deep breath and exhaling it slowly, she started at the beginning. "I told you, I don't know who I am. Everyone who knew is dead because I killed them. Well, more or less, I didn't kill Henry, but you get what I mean."

Michael nodded, giving her a small smile as she rolled on, "So, I lived in South America with the Dragons for about fifteen years that I can remember, and I was almost twenty before we hit the road. I'm positive about this because Henry and all the rest of the Dragons attested to this. It was a known fact."

Michael pursed his lips, trying to grasp why her age mattered.

"I was what you might call a late bloomer. This really pissed Eddie off because he was waiting for me to mature before we left the camp, and I was nearly eighteen before my body even started changing. He figured they couldn't take me on the road until I at least looked like a woman, or it would cause trouble." She slumped forward, pushing her elbows into her knees and her face into her hands.

"He acted like it was my fault or something, because it took so long for it to come. They pushed me so hard when I was young to make me strong and lay the foundation for my training. It was like my body was too busy to get around to it or something," she lamented.

She gave a lengthy pause, her mind trapped in the distant past. Michael ran his hand lightly across her back, waiting patiently for her to continue.

"Anyways," she finally picked the story up again, "When

the Feds formed the group to oversee my case, they had this Dr. Bennet, who kept telling them *'based on her bone structure, she's only fifteen,'* and I tried to call bullshit, but no one cared what I had to say. And since I had no proof, I lost," she finished looking defeated. "That's why I have to show the card, because I'm not completely free from the Feds."

Thinking about this for several minutes, Michael's mind returned to what Enrique had said about finding them; *he had help.* "Why do you suppose they did that?" he asked, a little short of breath.

"I dunno," her hunched shoulders indicating she didn't feel like talking any more.

Leaning forwards next to her, he wanted to be careful not to tip her off he had talked to her former lover. "No, No, No," he said rapidly, "Seriously. What did they gain by having you declared a minor? There had to be an advantage, or they wouldn't have gone to the trouble."

Tori shook her head for a moment, "You mean besides being able to send me to the halfway house for six months?" She shrugged her shoulders, "They couldn't have done that without it. That's how they tacked it onto our agreement."

At first, she wasn't seeing the point, continuing to stare at the floor. Then she looked at him sharply, sitting up straight in slow motion. Snapping her head towards the clerks counter, he could see the wheels spinning.

"Son of a bitch," she sputtered, "When we bought the garage, I showed them the card then. They've known where we are since we got here, even without getting my Driver's License. And now that cunt is back there notifying them we want to get married."

Michael still leaning forward, elbows to knees, looked back at her over his shoulder. "What should we do?" he asked, deferring to her judgment.

"What can we do?" she replied with a shrug, her eyes still on the counter. "I think they can keep us from getting married in the least, and could show up any time just to rattle my cage."

Michael had a bad feeling they already had, even if he had kept the visit to himself.

She clenched her jaw, the anger boiling inside her. *Why didn't I see this coming? And Eli, that lying bastard. I fell for it, hook, line and sinker.* She knew she'd been played; she had to give him that.

An uneasy feeling hung in the pit of her stomach. They wanted to control her; she had known that for a while. Whatever they had in mind, she wasn't going to give in so easily.

"We wait and see I guess. They haven't said 'no' yet, maybe they'll allow it," he tried to stay positive, giving her another smile.

Reaching up, she ran her fingers over him, her turn to do the rubbing. This should have been a happy day for them. Smiling back at him weakly, she tried to borrow some of his enthusiasm.

A short time later, the clerk returned and called them to the counter, their paperwork in hand. "Would you like a waiver?" she asked as she stamped the forms.

"A waiver? A waiver for what?" Michael had to ask.

"So you can see the judge," she calmly explained. "The normal waiting period is seventy-two hours from purchase to ceremony. I have been authorized to give you a waiver if you want this to be finalized today."

The couple shared a quick glance at one another before they spoke almost in unison, "Yes, we want a waiver." Michael could not help thinking, *authorized by whom?* He didn't dare ask.

The ceremony in the judge's chambers didn't take long,

and they were back outside with the clerk. She kept all of their paperwork and said they would get their official license in the mail in a few weeks. "Congratulations!" she called after them as they headed for the exit. Practically running down the steps, they turned for home, not stopping until they were safely inside the house.

Moving to the front window, Michael peeked outside, as if he were checking to see if they'd been followed. Tori burst into laughter at the sight, putting her arms around his neck. Leaning her forehead against his, they rocked side to side, breathing and enjoying the moment.

*Oh, my God*, she had the thought, *I know who I am.* Feeling breathless, she felt a warm flush covering her body; *I am Tori Anderson.* The name felt right to her, as if it had always been hers, and she could feel the butterflies dancing in her stomach, so happy she could cry.

Pushing her mouth forward, she began to kiss him. With slow, gentle movements, her hands caressed his neck and the back of his head, his hair soft between her fingers.

Parting his lips, Michael deepened the kiss, running his palms up and down her back, lost in his own desire. For a moment, he thought they might stay where they were, but on second thought he began to nudge her towards the back of the house, his excitement growing quickly out of control.

Making it into her bedroom, Tori remembered the harsh thoughts she had had about Michael and his pushing her to take the oversized bed. Looking at the ring on her finger, she remembered his message to her that lay against her skin, a tear slipping from her eye.

Catching it for her, he checked himself, asking in a whispery voice, "What's the matter?"

Shaking her head, she smiled broadly as she stroked him a few more times and then released him.

Taking a step back, she reached up and pulled the shirt

over her head. Immediately, he waved her off, taking over the job of removing her clothing. His hands moved slowly, his purpose sure. He then laid her naked form on the bed and removed his own shirt and boots for comfort. He leaned over the top of her, stroking her body with firm fingers, meant to convey his feelings for her.

Tori wasn't sure she could take it, breathing erratically, then catching his hands for a moment, "I don't like to be touched," she whispered. "It's almost more than I can bear."

Confused for a moment, Michael shook his head. "Just relax," he whispered. "I'm not gonna hurt you. I'm gonna make you feel real good. I promise."

Releasing him, Tori put her hands on her face and pushed her hair back, struggling to control the spasms that were shaking her body.

No one had ever touched her like that before, as it had always been her job to provide the pleasure, not to accept it. Taking slow deep breaths, she tried to be compliant, her lower lip quivering anxiously.

Michael worked his way down, kissing the soft line of her belly, taking his time to touch her arms and thighs, as well. When he reached the trimmed mat of hair that covered her folds of flesh, he rubbed his face against the tender area, his hands pushing against the inner part of her thighs to persuade her to shift them out and give him some room.

He blew gently against her delicate female parts, causing chills to ripple through her entire being. Using his tongue in ways she had never thought possible, he gave her more shudders as he worked, massaging the small bead that hid beneath the flesh. His hands were never still while he performed his magic, his palms sliding easily over every inch of skin he could reach.

Tori could feel her insides growing tense, a deep ache taking hold and she noticed she had become exceedingly moist inside of her warm hollow. After several minutes, Michael lifted his face, unfastening his jeans with an easy motion and dropping them to the floor. Holding himself above her, he teased her for a moment, his heart feeling like it would burst as he stared down into the eyes of his bride.

Leaning onto his elbows, he put his face down next to hers before dropping his hips and making his way inside her. She stiffened, not expecting it to hurt when he took her. Sensing her distress, he slowed his movement, pressing down with slow, steady pressure until he had taken her fully. His hands were comforting her; his lips kissing and nuzzling her face as he took things slow, allowing her to catch her breath.

Lying above her, Michael took his time, wanting her to know how much he treasured her. Kissing her and breathing heavily against her hairline, he made easy and deliberate movements before increasing his speed.

She began to moan and pant, accepting him more easily. Her own desire growing thicker, she wrapped her legs around him, then raised her feet towards the ceiling.

Catching her legs behind her knees, he pushed them down, folding her in half as he moved to drive her harder. He could feel himself losing control, unable to suppress the waves of need that were wracking his body.

He made loud groans, squeezing her skin in his palms, falling forward slightly as the spasms overtook him, and he released inside of her. She wrapped her arms around his head that lay against her, a great joy exploding inside her chest.

They lay together for several minutes in the awkward position, inhaling deeply and holding one another. Eventually, he allowed her legs to return to the bed and slid over next to her, pulling her onto her side with him. Snuggling into the crook of his arm, she laid her head on the side of his chest and ran the fingers of her left hand through the hairs playfully. Catching them, he surveyed the ring, noticing the perfect fit.

"How did you know what size to get?" she questioned him quietly as he entwined their fingers loosely.

"I asked Trish to get it for me. That's why she had the jewelry party after Christmas, so you could try some on, and she could get the size." He smiled at their sneakiness.

Pushing herself up on her elbow, she stared at him. "When exactly did you buy them?" she struggled to sound calm.

He stroked the hair away from her face, thinking for a moment, then replied coolly, "I ordered them the day I bought your guitar and brought you the roses."

Her jaw dropped slightly, "That was months ago, like, before Christmas," she stammered.

He smiled, giving her a small nod and using his arm to pull her in tightly. "Yup. I realized I wanted you almost as soon as we got here," he confessed, thinking *Mrs. Anderson* to himself.

# Make a Home

That night, they slept in each other's arms, like it had always been meant to be. Feeling his deep breaths next to her, she knew he had fallen asleep, and positioned herself so she could see his profile as the moonlight from the window fell across it. A handsome man, he was about thirty-five years old best she could recall. That would be about right; fifteen years younger than Henry, who would have been fifty that year.

A touch of sadness fluttered inside her heart as she remembered her husband's brother, the man who brought them together. Henry had sacrificed a great deal to give her a new life. She smiled as she realized she actually lay with the man he had spoken of that night in a diner; the one who would care for her. Kissing Michael's skin lightly, she knew that together, they would make a home. Resting her head against him, she drifted off to sleep.

Michael awoke early the next morning, amazed she still lay beside him. It was a rare day she did not rise before him. Her back turned to him, the sheet draped across the lower half of her. He could see the line of her back all the way down to her bare buttocks. Lying on her left side, the dark outline of her Dragon mark on her right shoulder was exposed. She had told him about the tattoo, but he had never seen it.

Tracing the outline of the small mark with his finger, he

leaned close enough to smell the scent of her. His chest pounded with excitement, realizing he was free to touch her. He was so glad he had not taken her before, as this was worth waiting for. She was his, but he didn't own her. Not the way other men had.

She was his equal, his partner, his love. He smiled, running his lips across her soft skin. She moved slightly as his breath brushed her warmly. He touched her more firmly, wishing for her to roll over and talk to him in her sweet low voice.

Spooning up behind her, he ran his hand around her waist and up the line of her front to cup her breast. She wasn't exceedingly large, but more than a handful. He liked the way she responded when he caressed her, leaning away from her so she could roll onto her back.

"Good morning," he greeted her in a low tone.

Not bothering to speak, she turned further, sliding on top of him, covering his mouth with her own. Now that he had awakened her, she could feel the craving to have him burning inside of her.

Her turn to do the pleasing, she was good at it, and had every intention of showing it. Her hands moved across his skin, leaving behind a blazing trail of desire. Sliding down, she straddled his legs so she could take him into her mouth, and he swelled up easily as she tantalized him with her tongue and lips. Pushing him down her throat, she worked him in and out, her soft folds leaking onto his legs as her body became enflamed by the taste of his salty ooze.

She ran her hands up to massage his belly, then down to squeeze his hips, continuing to drive him along for several minutes before sliding him out. Moving up so that she lay over him, she wasted no time taking him inside her, lying over so that her hardened nipples tickled his chest as she moved.

Running his hands up and down the length of her, he massaged the cheeks of her rear end, squeezing them gently as he followed her movements up and down on top of him. She ran her mouth across his chest, first breathing on his brown nipples, and then allowing her tongue to slide out and wet them as it danced lightly across the tops.

Pushing her up so that she sat on top of him, Michael used his hips to begin taking her more forcefully, and they found a rhythm as their bodies began coming together in a hard pounding motion. He could feel her growing tense, and wondered if he would last until she finished, when she began clutching at his hands that were roughly holding her up and preventing her from stretching out across him.

She began to make strange yelpish noises, and he held her firmly, the look on her face driving him on. Her jaw dropping and fingers curling, he realized he had made it, freeing him to allow his own fulfillment within her.

She lay across his chest and body as he deflated slowly, panting loudly. "Oh, my God," she managed in a hoarse whisper. "I feel so weak, like my palms are made of tingly jelly."

Michael smiled as he uncurled her fingers and kissed them lightly. "I love you," he told her softly.

Lifting her face, she smiled back, "I know," her eyes fluttering down to his lips and back up to his eyes, "I love you, too."

Her words gave him an incredible rush, confident she had never spoken them to anyone before. She wasn't that kind of girl, and would never have said them unless certain that she meant them.

Sliding his arms around her, he held on to her tightly, sobs of joy welling inside of him, as he ran his hands up and into her thick dark curls. A few minutes later, their strength had returned, and they climbed out of bed and into the shower together.

"You know," she confessed in a quiet voice, "I've been thinking about you a lot lately, especially when I have to listen to you in here alone."

He laughed, remembering his own provocative visions of her showers as of late. The warm water cascading over their bodies, he allowed his finger to trace the bite mark on her breast.

"I've been considering putting a tattoo over it. A cover that will last forever," she explained with a smile.

Nodding, he asked in a husky tone, "So, what're you gonna get?"

Touching it herself, she could feel the fire inside her flaring up again. "I haven't decided," she said in a weaker voice.

He returned her hungry glare, pushing her against the wall and lifting a leg to gain access to her warm interior. *Making love in the shower*, Michael grinned; *I like this*. Kissing her afterwards, he whispered, "You think it'll always be this way?"

She only smiled back, shutting off the water and reaching for a towel. They got dressed and had a late breakfast before they headed out to the garage to work on the bike for a bit. "I think I'm going to get a pink rose," she later said out of the blue.

Not grasping what she meant, he stopped to look at her, while she slid her hand over her breast, lightly massaging her old wound. "To cover it. A pink rose." Michael nodded his approval, and they closed up to have some lunch at the diner before taking his bike to the next town for a visit to the tattoo parlor there.

Walking into the café, they climbed into their usual seats and waited for Trish to make her way over to their table. "Hi guys," she started, "We wondered where you was yesterday.

The boys came back from yur place an' said you wasn't there after school."

A sliver of guilt ran through Michael's mind; they had forgotten the boys. He had begun to apologize, when she noticed the rings and squealed loudly, "Oh, my God! You guys got married, and you didn' invite me!" she teased them loudly.

Michael looked across the table at his wife, who wore a smile larger than he had known she owned. "We didn't actually invite anyone," he replied calmly, "It was more of a spur of the moment thing."

"Spur o' th' moment," she challenged in a playful manner, "Fur as long as you was plannin' it."

He laughed loudly, "I was planning, not that we were planning. Once I asked her, it kind of became… urgent." He could tell she wasn't really upset, and the mood remained light and cheerful as she took their order and went to put it in.

Reaching across the table, he played with Tori's fingers, so glad he could touch her. He would have asked if she were happy, but her face left no doubt as she sat in her usual quiet way. He liked that about her.

Enjoying the afternoon, they ate their meal in comfortable silence, and for a moment, Michael considered whether he should have told her about Enrique's visit. He wondered what her reaction might have been. He knew he wasn't going to mention it; it wasn't worth the risk of upsetting her.

Sliding onto his bike behind him, Tori relaxed against him and wrapped her arms around to lovingly massage his chest while they rode. From time to time, he would reach up to touch the back of her hands, his contentment evident. Pulling up in front of the tiny shop, they made their way inside and stopped at the counter.

Tori looked up at the wall behind it, examining the pictures closely. She knew exactly what she wanted. Not seeing it, she asked the tattoo covered man behind the glass if they had any rose pictures.

A shelf to the side of him stood covered in three ring binders, and he slid his pudgy finger along the spines until he found the one he wanted. Pulling it out, he laid it on the counter for her to browse. Slowly turning the pages she became engrossed, giving Michael a chance to look around the shop.

Seeing the variety of artwork available, an idea occurred to him, and he turned, walking around the room and going over the designs on the walls until he found the one he wanted. Sideling up next to her, back over at the counter, Tori had found the one she desired and pulled down her shirt by the neck to show the guy the bite she wanted it to cover.

Eyeing her breast and the nonchalant way she had exposed it for him, he nodded his agreement, and that it could be done. Another equally marked man came to take her to the back and begin the process.

As soon as she exited the room, presumably out of earshot, Michael announced, "I wanna get one too. I want it to go in the same spot as hers, but I want that motorcycle over there," he indicated the photo, "And I want TORI underneath it."

The man spewed a surly laugh, and Michael looked confused, "Is there something wrong with that?" his voice slightly angry.

"No man, just always amazed when people put other people's names on their bodies. As if their love's gonna last forever. You get what you want, man; it don' matter to me."

*Real philosophical*, Michael observed to himself; *jackass.*

They both kept their new marks covered until the evening, when they were getting ready for bed. Michael showed her his first, as he felt especially proud of the way it had turned out. It wasn't very large, only about four inches across, but the guy had done a fantastic job, and once it had healed, it would be perfect hiding inside the hair on his chest.

Tori appeared pleased when she saw her name etched in his skin, it causing her heart to pound that she meant that much to him. On her breast, she wore a new pink rose, which covered the reddish circular scar of teeth marks perfectly, and she displayed it for her mate with pride.

Staring at it, Michael moved closer and turned her, as he noticed something odd about one of the shadowed sides. Gently lifting her to catch the light better, he could see the letters MICHAEL worked into the edges of the petals. "So that's what he meant," he commented while grinning broadly.

Their love rough that night, the adrenaline of the day made them anxious. He enjoyed the feel of her and the way she moaned when he drove himself against her. He finished her again before him, and she breathed in deeply when she whispered how incredible it had been as they were drifting off to sleep.

Michael only smiled, kissing her neck while toying with her hair. Enrique's visit still loomed in the back of his mind, and he wondered how long they would have before the other shoe fell.

# Safe Place

The couple had been married a few weeks, and things were going smoothly. They had settled into a routine of sorts; early to bed, late to sleep. They both got up at 5:00 am to make a short run and exercise, and then returned home to enjoy one another's sweaty bodies before their shower and starting the day. Michael loved to watch the way she moved; when she was naked, when she was dressed, either way.

He took every chance he could get to touch her, having been denied for so long. He had never been in love like this, and he knew it was the same for her. He still wanted to learn more about the bikes, and she became more patient than ever as she explained new processes to him and gave him the chance to use his hands to try on his own, observing as he worked. He liked that she watched him, making him warm inside.

Steven and Chris continued to come over every day, still having another month before school ended. Tori gave them lessons, teaching them to play the guitar when they didn't have school work, and Michael thoroughly enjoyed watching and listening. He had worked for *Indelible* over four years; he knew what good music sounded like. Hers was more than good. Sometimes, he would allow himself to wonder if she would've been a musician in her original life.

Michael could feel himself becoming obsessed with her true identity. It bothered him that the Feds had gone to such lengths to obscure her age, and wondered if they secretly knew who she was, but hid it for some dark purpose. She had told him about her skills and having been created as some kind of secret weapon, and this bothered him deeply, as if it were only a matter of time before her past would find them.

He never mentioned Enrique's visit to her, but it troubled him, as well. He remembered what the man had said about giving her his number, so when he noticed her wallet lying out while she showered, he picked it up to peek inside. Sure enough, he found the worn pink piece of paper folded in its place, and he felt tempted to remove it to dispose of the issue once and for all.

Quietly, he ran his finger across the ink. He considered the fact that she still held on to it, and wondered if she ever thought about the dark haired man who had sat across from him the morning she took his name.

Shaking the thought from his mind, Michael had closed the wallet and left the paper inside. Enrique was her ghost, not his, and she the one who would have to discard the past when it was time. He tried not to think about it any further, but it remained difficult, knowing the man obviously wanted her back.

One particular Sunday, a short time after that, he had asked her something about her first memories, and she had opened up about it a bit more than ever before. It pleased him that she felt she could trust him, and had become willing to share.

They were seated on the couch, her guitar across her lap. "I had an amazing childhood," she began as she caressed her beloved gift. "My first memory is of living in the rainforest in Brazil. It was a beautiful place, and I loved my life in the camp, with Henry and the others; free to roam the jungle and explore the world through the books that were given to me."

Looking over at her book cases, he knew what she meant,

as they were already gathering quite a collection of volumes.

"Those guys were so patient, never tired of my questions, always ready to tell me about things or share a story, or whatever I needed." Tori looked out the window for a moment before she continued. *There's so much to tell, and still so much to hide.*

When she was young, they spent their time preparing her, teaching her what she would need to know for later. Brian, her physical mentor, taught her to be strong and cunning. Bill had been in charge of math and science lessons, ensuring she had a strong foundation. Henry taught her history and art, and Marcus languages, writing and problem solving.

Each man had a part to play, each building a portion of her knowledge, and she learned because of her curiosity and eagerness to know more. Most of all, she liked to please them. Sometimes, their lessons overlapped, as all of them shared what they knew, each of them wanting her to be most like them. Tori never questioned their motives, as she loved her early life and accepted it at face value.

In addition to the group who lived in the camp with her year round, there were some who came and went with the seasons. When they left, Tori seldom thought about where they were off to or what they were doing. They were not her favorites, she explained, and she had no interest in the bikes they rode or the life that they lived. She felt happy with the four men who spent the most time with her. They were her family, more so than any of the others.

Eddie, leader of the Dragons, rode with the traveling group. He came into camp to keep track of her and her studies, and was waiting for the time to be right for her to begin the next phase of her education, which would be his part. He had also claimed to be her father, but they were not close, and she never believed it to be true.

Henry was the one who did his best to nurture her and

taught her how to take care of herself. For many years, he bathed her and washed her hair, teaching her how to be clean and how to handle life's little problems. And he taught her to play the guitar; she couldn't forget that, and smiled wistfully as she spoke of it.

In the end, it was Henry who brushed her long ebony locks, washed her clothes, and cared for her physical needs. There were others who lived in the camp with them, but these were jobs that only Henry did.

Michael smiled at hearing how his brother had nurtured her. Remembering how it had felt like she had been made for him, he couldn't help thinking that maybe she had been, and Henry had wanted them to be a couple after all.

Tori explained that she didn't like Eddie's visits to the camp. He often would hit or kick her in anger, or for no reason at all, and had done so ever since she could remember. Definitely not a patient man, he sometimes touched her in ways that made her uncomfortable. "You know, nothing bad or anything. It seemed like he wanted to hug on me, or for me to want to be around him, but I didn't because I didn't like him. I thought he was mean, so I avoided him."

Tori felt guilty when she admitted that every time Eddie left the camp, she would hope he would never return. "I'm not sure that I wanted him to die. I only wished he wasn't part of my life, and certainly didn't want to believe he could be my father."

"He was waiting for me to mature, and I hoped that would never happen either, but eventually it did... like my body went crazy. It was really hard for me," she elaborated, "I had never been around a woman before, and suddenly I started growing in weird places and getting hair and the only people I had to talk to were men. But Henry noticed, and he had some books for me, like he knew I would need them or something, and he answered my questions if I had the courage to ask. It worked out."

"I hated getting my periods though," she confessed. "That was the worst. I couldn't see why God made me a girl. So not fair."

Michael laughed, "I'm glad he made you a girl," he teased. Reaching over, he ran his hand up and down her thigh, giving her a squeeze of encouragement. "I'm glad you're able to share this with me, but I'm ok if you don't."

Tori nodded her appreciation, but having started the conversation, she wanted to do her best to finish it. She swallowed hard, coming to the parts that would be the most difficult to share. As her body finished developing, Tori became curious about the men around her. They were different from her, and she seemed to hate that she wasn't one of them, "But I got used to it," she declared. "Got a little fantasy thing going for a while, thinking about what sex might be like."

She paused for a minute to reflect, looking at her lap, "No one touched me back then, but I still remember thinking after the first time that it wasn't anything like I had expected. But that wasn't until just before we hit the road, so let me back up a bit."

"Let's see… When Eddie and the rest of the group came back to camp that year, after I finally started to change, he commented on how I had filled out since he'd been gone. That gave me chills, because I didn't ever want that man to touch me, him or Red, either one."

"So, I really looked forward to their going back out again, but this time they didn't go. They stayed at the camp, leaving their bikes in storage and hanging out with us all the way up until we all left together. That's when those of us who had been living at the camp became regular members of the Dragons." She paused again, pinching and rubbing her lips for a moment while she collected her thoughts.

"It was during that last couple of years or so that they really put the final touches on my training. Taught me how to do some really bad shit. Guns, knives, a little bit about explosives and what not. I still didn't get what for. Don't get me wrong, I knew the Dragons were bad guys; I had been around them all my life, and it would've been hard to miss. I just didn't know how bad. Or what was coming." She looked a little forlorn, knowing how dark things were going to get in hindsight.

"I got good at it though. Henry and I were about the same height, and Brian had made me strong. Then Eddie started teaching me how to fight, and that was something I took to. I kept telling myself if I got good enough, someday I would be able to beat him, instead of him always beating on me."

She gave a cynical grin, "A lot of it came down to my fault though. Guess you could say I brought it on myself, being stubborn and making bad choices sometimes. That's how he got me most of the time; he would keep hitting me until I finally had enough and gave in."

"So anyways, we finished up my training there at the camp, and we only had one last thing to establish. See, Eddie had this plan, how I would be traveling with the group, only no one outside would know I was really part of them, like a regular member, so I would be somehow hidden or some shit. He called me a secret weapon later on, and suddenly all this shit that happened at the camp made sense, you know? So here Eddie says it's time for us to get ready to leave, and we need to get me ready for being out on the road."

"He sent Paul and David to go get clothes for me, and I was pissed because I didn't want to go on the road with them, or wear their stupid uniform, or any of that crap. I go to find Henry and I tell him I want to stay in the camp with him." She smiled at the memory of Henry's reaction to her demands.

"He held me for a few minutes, rocking me back and forth like he used to when I was little, but then he says something weird. *'I have to be careful, baby girl. Eddie wants to be your first.'* He said it just like that, and then he walked away, and I had no idea what he meant." She bit her lip.

"But," Michael interrupted, "I thought you said Henry was your first."

"Oh, he was," she clarified with a shy smile, feeling the color deepen in her cheeks. "Yeah, and you know that really pissed Eddie off. That's why he kept Henry from touching me; I think so anyways."

"We made love that night in his hammock; the only time a man touched me with respect, until Eli. Only now I realize what happened with Eli was just a game. Damn it." She looked angry as she recalled the events and time she spent with the latter.

She gave a lengthy pause, and Michael pondered what she had told him carefully. "So what was your secret job then, making hits for the group?" Michael had been Special Forces, like his brother, and he had a suspicion their motives were far darker than what she had shared. "I mean, you did perform in that capacity."

Nodding slowly, she agreed as the numerous victims she had taken became a wash before her. "I guess you could say, I've done my best to forget, but it still hurts that I hadn't been strong enough to say no."

"You know those people would've died either way. You know that, right?" Michael tried to console her. "If you hadn't been the one to act, one of the other team members would have. The outcome would have been the same, regardless of who held the knife or pulled the trigger or what have you."

"Have you ever killed anyone?" she asked him in a soft

voice.

Taken by surprise, Michael looked at his hands. It had been a long time, but sometimes he still felt the guilt. "I did what I had to do," he replied slowly, "We always do, right?" He gave her a half smile as he shifted his eyes to look into hers. "I wish I could say the pain goes away. It gets easier, but I'm not sure it ever totally leaves you."

Sliding her guitar off the end of the couch, she climbed over onto his lap and sat facing him. Placing her left hand behind his neck to massage the edge of his hairline, she ran her right hand through the hair along the side of his head. At the same time, Michael ran his own hands up and down the length of her back in a comforting fashion, sitting and looking into each other's souls.

# Hidden Agendas

Sitting so comfortably with her, Michael felt the temptation to wipe away the conversation as he rubbed his hands over her warm flesh. He loved being with her, and it was a fine afternoon for such a thing. Kissing her deeply, he could feel the nag in the back of his mind, and he knew he wasn't ready to give up on sorting things out if she were ready to share.

Staring into her eyes as she sat on his lap, he pushed for more. "Tell me about your secret job then. Do you think it was making the hits, or more than that?"

She drew a deep breath, reluctantly sliding back to her seat next to him, but remaining close enough to massage his chest as she spoke.

"I'm really scared it was more than that," she admitted quietly. "So much happened that I wasn't privy to, so many hidden agendas. Like The Organization. All of that shit was deep dark secret, but Eddie was getting me access bit by bit. Teaching me things or telling me to find out things. I didn't give all that stuff to the Feds, either; and looking back I'm really glad I kept it to myself."

Remembering her weapons, she inhaled sharply and tucked her sock covered feet underneath her. "You remember my pistol and knife? The ones I have now? They knew I had those," she poked his chest firmly as she spoke. "I told them when I was arrested for beating up those thugs, told Jim

Godfry I had them and where to find them. He let me walk out of the police station with the knife in my pocket and he never did anything about the Beretta. Don't you think that's odd?"

Michael quickly agreed, "I think it's more than odd." Sliding his arm behind her, he pulled her close, "I'm gonna look out for you the best I can. I love you so much," he whispered into her hair.

She clung to him for several minutes, her heart thumping in her ears. She loved him too, and cursed Terry for being right and herself for not believing him.

Sliding back onto his lap, she began kissing him more demandingly, and although he seemed to want to continue the conversation, she no longer cared to talk about the past. Pulling her shirt off in a quick, excited motion, she ran her hands across his chest, and he watched the pink flower as it rose and fell on the side of her left breast.

Michael loved the fact she had put his name over Eddie's scar. Running his hands up and down her back, he could feel himself expanding in his tight jeans, with her warm hollow pressing down on him through the fabric. He made love to her every day, two or three times a day and still it wasn't enough. Either she was insatiable, or he was.

Their petting grew heavy, and he lifted her off of himself, laying her down onto the living room floor. Grasping the front of her pants, he opened the fly and slid them off of her cleanly shaven legs. He enjoyed the way she always kept herself smooth and groomed for him. He grinned mischievously as his fingers slid across the short hairs that covered her folds of skin.

Bending over, he used his mouth to satisfy her, and she clawed at his head and shoulders as he finished her. He found her to be dripping wet when he finally removed his own clothing and sank his hardness deep inside her. She made loud noises as he drove her on the carpet, completely submissive to his need, and for a moment he wondered if she really had enjoyed what the men who came before him did to her. He lay over her panting heavily as he recovered, almost certain he would never find out.

The couple had exited the shower and were getting dressed when there came a loud knock on their front door. Surprised, Michael left her to finish making herself decent while he went to see who it could be, visiting on a Sunday. He returned to her a few minutes later, telling her to put on her makeup, as they had been requested at the diner.

She eyed him with suspicion, but he only shrugged, and they finished dressing before walking down the street in the early evening sun. Reaching the door, they were greeted by a crazy and joyous surprise inside. Virtually everyone they knew waited within the café, eager to give the couple a proper wedding reception.

Michael could see the shocked surprise on her face as Tori's eyes swept around the room. He smiled broadly at her when she walked over to the tall white cake that sat on a table, wanting to inspect the tiny figures that rested on the top.

She cracked a small grin as she noticed how the couple resembled her husband and herself. Sliding her hand into his, she looked sheepishly at the floor, realizing everyone knew how she felt. It was harder for her than she would have thought, not feeling like she owned her feelings anymore, now that they were public.

In addition to the cake, they had food to eat and gifts for the young couple. The pair opened them together, making sure to thank each giver loudly. Michael enjoyed the warm flush on her face, her pleasure at receiving the attention obvious. By nightfall, it had been a well spent day, and they had no doubt they were respected members of the community in which they lived.

Seeing Tori head off for a visit with Trish, Michael decided to have a quick word with Marge, who sat alone in a booth. Sliding into the opposite side, he greeted her with a grin, "And how have you been?"

Marge looked surprised by his warm gesture, and smiled slightly as she replied, "I been gettin' by."

Nodding, he informed her, "You should come by sometime, see what Tori and I have done with the place."

She gave him a reassuring nod, telling him, "I jus' might have t' do that."

At that moment, Tori made her way over to take a seat next to him, and she smiled at the older woman, but did not speak. Taking her husband's hand, she squeezed it firmly, and sat looking into his eyes.

"You sure are a quiet one," Marge commented as she observed the newlyweds. "You know it was you who convinced Georgie t' sell you that place."

Tori looked at her with a raised brow, pretending she didn't know what the woman was talking about, so Marge elaborated, "That day you came t' the house. Somethin' about the way you begged him convinced him t' sell you th' garage. Afterwards, he'd go down an' watch th' two o' you while you worked so hard on it, happy with what he saw. It meant a lot t' him that you was breathin' life back int' somethin' he had spent s' much o' his own t' build. It brought him a lot o' joy those las' few months."

Michael could not help thinking what a sweet woman she really was. George had been a lucky man. Kissing the back of Tori's hand, he whispered, "We better go," and the couple said goodnight to the older woman before making a brief speech of thanks and excusing themselves to head home.

The next few days went by quietly, and school let out for the last time. Summer in a small town, the couple couldn't have been happier on the surface. Inside, they both could feel the darkness coming. Lying awake after making love in the June night air, Tori massaged the hair on his chest, toying with her name, while Michael appeared lost in thought. "What're you thinking?" she asked quietly, seeing that he wasn't really with her.

Coming back with a small shake of his head, he replied, "I'm thinking we should close everything up and make a road trip. I dunno," he gave a small shrug of his broad shoulders, "Someplace we don't buy anything. We still have lots of money, and we have been pretty successful with the bikes. You do a fantastic job on them, and we get top dollar."

"We do a fantastic job," she corrected him, adjusting the sheets. "So where are we going?" she asked as if the decision had already been made. "Take your bike and just head out?"

He nodded his agreement, "Maybe. I think we need to be away from here. Like we've stayed in one place for too long. You kept $50k in cash; we could live on the road a long time on that."

Silently, she had to agree, as the tension around them seemed almost palpable many days. They both ignored it the best they could, but in the end, they both knew it was there. And they would always have their home to come back to when they were ready. Drifting off to sleep, they each thought about what was coming, whether they wanted it to or not.

The next morning, Michael helped her clean up the shop extra well. They put all the tools away where they would be waiting for their return. Washing the sheets on the bed and packing up things inside the house, Tori hid her guitar inside a closet, rubbing it fondly as she remembered how he had given it to her on Christmas morning.

It had been the most special gift, and tears touched her eyes at having to leave it behind. When she could not find the words to express her feelings, she could always rely on it to set her spirit free, and she would miss it as the dearest of friends.

Throwing their clothes into their backpacks for them, they would have two changes each. Tori smiled, knowing things would be different traveling with Michael. She felt relieved her nightly duties would be something she wanted to do and rather enjoyed. Twisting her ring that held his message of love pressed against her finger, she smiled with elation. Looking around as she gave the house one last inspection on the way out, she locked the door and trotted back into the shop, carrying their packs.

Walking in quick strides, she realized most people would have been heartbroken to have to leave their home under such circumstances. How odd that she would be almost giddy at the prospect of riding across the country, just the two of them.

She had never been one for worldly possessions. He was the thing that meant the most to her, and therefore she had all she would ever need when he was with her.

Turning from the office into the garage, she stopped cold at the sight that lay before her. Michael stood waiting there, looking at the floor, Special Agent Eli Founder beside him.

Seeing her come in, Eli looked over and a small smile spread across his lips. "Hello," he spoke in a quiet, patronizing voice.

Dropping the bags, she did not return the greeting. Staring at him icily, she crept up to her husband and slid her arm around his waist in a protective manner.

Michael gazed over at her, his heart racing as she looked him in the eye. Only an inch or so shorter than him, he leaned his forehead easily against hers and closed his eyes as she held him.

*We should have left yesterday,* he thought to himself. Slipping his arm around her as well, he whispered, "It's gonna be ok."

Eli cleared his throat nervously, indicating they should break it up. The couple ignored him, having no respect for the man. Pushing harder, he said in a demanding voice, "Can I have a word alone with her now, please?"

Loosening his grip enough to turn and face him, Michael could feel his face flush, "No, you can't."

Eli gave him an angry glare, so he let loose with a controlled tirade, "No, you may not speak to my wife in private. Whatever you have to say, you can say in front of me, or you don't need to say it. I don't know what game you and your people are playing, but we both know you're toying with her. You can't just erase a decade of someone's life because it suits you. I know why you did it, so you could keep tabs on her better, control her a little more. Whatever you want, she's not doing it."

Eli only stared at him calmly. *She'll do what we need her to do, one way or the other.* Aloud, he countered, "You don't really have a choice. I'm here under orders to escort you to New York. We have an urgent matter there and need you. *Now.*" He spoke the last word with a threatening tone, his body growing stiff.

Shifting his gaze out into the street, Michael could see Eli had not come alone. Considering their options, he ran his hand up and down her back in a slow circular motion. Using their German, he asked her in a low tone, "What do you think?"

She drew a ragged breath, still clinging to him and whispered in kind, "I think we're going to New York."

Nodding, he told Eli they needed to lock up. They grabbed their packs and followed him to the car that awaited out front. Looking down the narrow street, he wished they had had the chance to explain things to Trish, as he could see the small group of federal agents and pair of black cars had not gone unnoticed in the small town.

Before placing them into the back seat, Eli asked for her weapons, and Tori pulled them out of her bag to hand them to him, a sour expression on her delicate features. Placing the couple inside the vehicle, he made his way around to the passenger side to climb in himself. Michael smiled at the fact that he had disarmed her, perhaps afraid she would use them to escape; in essence, they were scared of her.

Looking back at their shop, he had a stab of sadness at the realization they may never see it again. Laying his arm on the seat behind her, he knew that the most important thing sat beside him. They were permitted to be alone in the rear compartment and rode comfortably in silence, allowing their fingers to say what needed to be said.

It took a couple of hours for them to arrive in San Antonio, where they would board a non-stop flight to New York. Stopping at a small eatery, they were allowed to have a meal while they waited for the time to board the plane. Tori had only been on a plane the one time she flew from Chicago to LA, and the prospect began to make her tense.

Michael held her close to him, loving the way she felt in his arms. They had shared a few months together in peace, and he knew it had been more than she had ever had before. But, like the eye of a hurricane, the calm doesn't last for long. Silently, he hoped they would be able to return when whatever this turned out to be had ended. If they did, he intended make Marge an offer to buy her old house.

He and Tori might not be able to make babies, but that didn't mean they couldn't adopt a few. He had the urge to have a real family with the girl, and would be eager to run it by her when the time was right.

When it came time for them to board, Eli walked beside her in silence, but he could feel the ache in his chest. Giving Michael an angry look, jealousy raged inside him.

Michael gave him an icy glare as they moved to take their seats. By their body language, their hatred for one another would have only been clearer if they had begun exchanging blows.

Seeing the stares and sensing the tension, Tori had never had to deal with anything like this. She felt at a loss as to what she should do. Watching her mate helplessly, she only hoped he knew how much she truly loved him.

Making it onto the plane, they located their seats in the center row. Michael then realized he had no desire to sit next to the man who had used his love so heartlessly, but on the other hand he didn't want her to sit next to him either. The dilemma tore at him on the inside, and he suggested in an even tone, "Hey, why don't you take a seat someplace else. Neither of us cares to share your company."

Ignoring him, Eli spoke to her in French. "Look," he said quietly, "I really would like to speak to you. Just for a few minutes. I have some things I need to clear up."

Shooting him a seething stare, "Guilty conscience?" she asked coldly.

Taken aback, he shook his head, and then began in a flat tone. "You know, you can be angry all you want. What happened between us wasn't entirely my fault. I asked you to go to your room, remember?" He pointed his finger at her and around in the air as he spoke, indicating the room he had wanted to send her to. He spoke more loudly, still in French, and people were beginning to stare.

"You chose to stay, you wanted to be there. Don't act all high and mighty, miss innocent, because we both know you're not." His words were sharp with rage on the verge of breaking loose.

Quietly, she said they should take their seats and stop drawing attention, looking around anxiously at all the eyes that were on them.

Michael glared at Eli, his eyes like daggers; he wanted to beat the hell out of him at that moment, all she had to do was give the word.

Tori sat down, and following her lead, Michael took the seat to her right. Eli took the seat to her left, adjusting his tie and straightening his suit. She stared straight ahead, keenly aware that Eli might have tried to keep his words between them, but as Michael was fluent in French as well, he had understood every word that had been spoken. It was going to be a long five hours.

Feeling the plane taxi to the runway, Michael could see Tori's face tense. Sensing her trepidation, he looped his fingers with hers and kissed her hand lovingly. "It's ok," he whispered, "Nothing to be afraid of."

Eli's head snapped to look at him, but Tori obstructed his view.

Michael grinned to himself; he had won either way, as she was wearing his ring, not Eli's.

After the plane leveled out, Tori gave Michael's hand a squeeze, and they shared a deep kiss, causing the man to her left to squirm. She had wanted to establish where her loyalties lay before she continued the conversation with the man who had used her.

Turning towards him after the kiss ended, she spoke in a low tone, maintaining the French. Michael could still hear, but at least the conversation would stay amongst the three of them more than likely.

"Ok," she admitted quietly, "I'm not innocent. Far from it. And I did want what happened between us at the time."

She stared at her lap as she spoke. "But you knew the Feds were playing games with me. Are still playing games with me. I trusted you. You don't have any remorse for that?" Tori looked up at him, his blue eyes watching her as she laid the guilt on him.

Swallowing, he nodded slightly, and replied curtly, "I was doing my job."

She cut in sharply, "Were you still doing your job the night you laid with me? I don't get it Eli. You wrote that message to me in the fairy tale book. You made it sound like you loved me, like you were going to be waiting for me. You have no idea how much it hurt when I realized you weren't in Chicago anymore, and it was all a lie."

Michael saw the tear as it spilled over and ran down her cheek, his gut wrenching at her sadness. Holding her digits firmly, he tried to comfort her, letting her know he was still there for her.

She allowed her thumb to rub lightly across the back of his hand, taking solace in the support he gave her. He knew this had been painful for her, and she felt grateful for him and his understanding.

"I never said I loved you," Eli tried to justify his actions. "I played the role I was given. I was to get close to you, and I did that. I was to get information from you, and I did that. That night cost me my position. When the agency found out you spent the night at my place and not the hospital, I got reassigned. Debra was reprimanded as well, for helping me."

"But you weren't charged with anything, because I was right about my age." She spit the words at him in disgust.

Rolling his eyes, he hem and hawed, "Technically we don't know. I mean sure, you're older than Dr. Bennet let on, but since your identity is still not certain, no one really knows." Looking at his hands, he acquiesced, "I would say your guess would be pretty close; off the record of course."

His confession did not bring her the satisfaction she had hoped for. "So why the lie? Why the deception?" She wrinkled her face as she spoke, "I don't get it Eli, why would you do all of this to me while pretending you were helping me?" She held her rage in check, but angry tears were still forming in her tender blue eyes.

"It did help you. Being younger helped get the deal we cut you. It made you appear less involved and more of a victim in the crimes of the Dragons –"

Tori cut him off, "And it meant you could watch me closer and send me to the halfway house and all of that other shit, too. It still gave you control over me you shouldn't or wouldn't have had."

Looking at her again, he agreed offhandedly, with a silent waft of his hand.

Tori's expression changed, another darker purpose occurring to her, "And it means you didn't find out who I am… because you didn't go far enough back." Eli looked at her with a stoic expression. "You didn't find my family, because you didn't want to."

Michael silently agreed; they had never intended to find her identity. She was right; changing her age helped them accomplish that goal, as well.

Eli looked even more uncomfortable, as if he knew some other dark portion of the story he wasn't going to tell her yet, and hoped she didn't guess. Her intuition had always been scary at times.

Staring at him, her eyes swimming with distrust, Tori hated to think what it could possibly be.

# Sneak Peek at Exposed

## Book 4 of A New Life Series

"Whaddaya think? Is he tellin' th' truth?" Buck leaned against the support pole, waiting to see what would be their next move.

Brett ran his fingers over his lips, studying the man hanging from the roof in front of them. "Unlikely."

"Want I should beat some sense int' 'im?" he grinned, reaching for his shiny buckle.

"You fat bastard! You really thinks my story's gonna change? Cut me down, le's settle this like men... see how many more teeth you can come up missin'," their victim growled angrily, blood dripping from his chin.

Buck stared back, waiting for his leader to give the word.

"Light him up," Brett muttered and turned to walk away, pulling a cigarette from his pocket with one hand and digging for his Zippo with the other. He could hear the sound of the leather as it ripped into Enrique's flesh. *Damn things are gonna kill me*, he coughed, flipping the lighter closed with a flick of his wrist.

Crushing out the butt beneath the heel of his boot a few minutes later, he made his way back over to their prisoner. Surveying the fresh wounds that oozed blood down his back, he released a low whistle. "Buck, my friend, I think you enjoy that belt o' yurs too much."

Shifting so that he could make eye contact, "You come

191

up with anything yet? You know I should kill you. All you gotta do is tell me where to find 'er, an' you get to live. Now, don't that sound like a heck of a good deal?"

"I told you," Enrique's chest heaved as he struggled to breathe, "I dunno where she's at... Calls me stupid fur tryin' t' play... you boys like I did... I ain't seen her... since the Dragons was here... swear to God."

"Ya know, I never thought you's a smart man. But even yur not dumbfuck enough to call me up an' tell me you're bringin' me Eddie's prize whore, when ya got no fuckin' clue where she's at!" Brett's voice had been slowly escalating in volume, ending in a full shout, "Tell me where the fuck she is, God dammit!" For emphasis, he kicked his former group mate in the ribs with his knee to punctuate his curses.

Enrique fell into a spasm of coughs, a wad of phlegm and blood spewing out onto the ground in front of him. "Kill me then..." he heaved, "I gots nothin' else to say."

Brett punched him in the ear, scowling in his rage. Turning to storm away, he ran his hand through his curly red hair. Motioning to Buck, "Le's talk."

The pair made their way down the road a couple of hundred yards, well out of earshot of any of the others. "We ain't gettin' nothin' from him. Even if he knows, he ain't gonna tell us." Brett inhaled deeply, blowing the air out through pursed lips. "We need another plan."

"We gonna kill 'im?" Buck tossed his thumb over his shoulder, towards the metal awning, "Or jus' let 'im 'ang till someone finds 'im?"

"Naw, we cut him down. I have another way to find her... jus' may not work's all. Depends on what she knows. Worth a shot though, our only shot really."

Half an hour later, Enrique sat on the stone bench, his gear strewn on the table behind him. His ears were ringing something fierce, and his body ached from the worst beating he had ever taken, but he refused to let them think they'd won. "I guess you believes me now?" he demanded in a surly tone.

"Naw, I think you're a liar. But tha's ok. We're gonna find 'er. An' when we do, I'm gonna give 'er the same beatin' I jus' gave you, jus' t' be fair."

Enrique's head shot up to see Buck sneering down at him. "See? I knew you's lyin'. I sees it in yur eyes, boy. So I make a deal wit ya… you find 'er, an' you bring 'er in, an' I won't make 'er bleed when I lay int' 'er." Buck grinned at him, his tongue pushed through the gaps of his missing teeth in an excited fashion.

Enrique breathed deeply, his mind spinning. Dropping his gaze to stare at the boots of the man in front of him, his heart pounded inside his chest. Taking in ragged breaths, he kept his head down, not daring to look up as the footwear turned and walked away from him. He cringed as he heard the sound of the bikes start up around him and head off down the road, leaving him in a cloud of dust, alone in the late afternoon sun.

# What Awaits

Tori sat between the two men in silence. On her right sat her husband, the man of her dreams. *Hell, it could be anyone's dreams really; he's tall, dark and handsome, right?* However, he's also supportive, intelligent and protective - everything a girl could want in a man.

On her left sat her former lover. He's short, conniving, and deceitful. *A man who has lied to me, used me and sent me on my way. So why am I feeling so conflicted?* It had been a year since she had even seen Eli, and so much had happened since then.

Stealing a glance at the man to her left, she noticed his intense glare, boring into the seat in front of him. His brows were furrowed, jaw clenched, obviously deep in angry thought. Allowing her mind to drag the memories of him to the surface, she recalled the first time she had ever seen him, pressing her down into the mattress of a hospital bed to restrain her. *I can still smell the gel in his hair as he held me there.*

She had just regained consciousness after murdering eleven men in a farmhouse in Iowa. That, and she had tried to kill herself. That's what all the liquor had been for; so that she would go to sleep and never have to face another day, filled with the guilt that still haunts her. *Thank God it hadn't worked.*

In the days that followed, Eli had come to visit her. He wanted her to talk, but she wasn't ready for that yet. Wasn't ready to feel and be and live. The hurt was too raw, too new, and all she could do was listen; so he talked.

He shared so much about himself, gave her so much attention. And it wasn't big things either. The little things he did mattered the most; those little cherished moments that stole her heart.

His little book of fairy tales, his little pink rose. He wanted something from her, but he got more than he expected. *He's right. You wanted to be in his bed that night, to make love to him,* she remembered their passion fondly. But she had never been cared for before, never given dignity, so she didn't know any better. He did. *He knew it was wrong. He should have put a stop to it.*

Giving her head a shake to clear it, she swung her gaze away from him. Holding Michael's hand, his fingers entwined with her right and covered by her left, she stroked him with her thumb affectionately.

Staring down at the shiny white gold on her special finger, she recalled how he had walked into her life and how hard she had worked to push him out of it. *God, I hated his being there.* At least at first she did.

Exposed is Available Now!

# About the Author

Anyone who knows me could tell you, I am a friendly kind of person, never met a stranger and take up conversations anywhere at any time. I work hard, and my mind never seems to shut down, as I wake up often in the middle of the night with ideas pouring out and demanding to be dealt with. Of course that means much of my books were written in the middle of the night.

I grew up and still live in the great state of Texas where everything is bigger, where we have warm weather and a central location. I love my state, my town, and my family, which includes my four sons, my significant other, and many friends as well.

I have thoroughly enjoyed writing this story and hope that you will love reading it just as much. And of course, there will be many more adventures to come.

You can follow Samantha Jacobey at:
Website: www.SamJacobey.com
Facebook: https://www.facebook.com/SamJacobey
Twitter: https://twitter.com/SamJacobey
Pinterest: http://www.pinterest.com/samanthajacobey/

# Other works by Samantha Jacobey

http://www.amazon.com/-/e/B00GEB5LX0

**Summer Spirit Novella Series** - no one EVER had a summer romance like this... Charlie visits another plane, parallel to our own, where Summer Angels and Dark Angels battle over the fate of man. A unique twist on an old idea that will keep you guessing; will Charlie and Clarisse ever find their HEA? (New adult)

**Irrevocable Series** – from affluent beginnings, BAILEY DEWITT's life has become a broken mess... after her parents died unexpectedly, she didn't think it could get any worse. But when the arrogance of man catches up and puts the entire world into a dooms-day spiral, there will be only ONE PLACE she can run to... the ONE PLACE she wanted desperately to escape.... (New Adult)

**Teach Me to Prey** – in this standalone thriller, JASON TRUITT and his friends have gotten their way for years. Deceit, sex, and foul play aren't normally covered in the curriculum, but they're doing whatever it takes to get under BECKY STEWART's skin. When one of the boys turns up dead, it's a race against time to save the others; a STUNNING STORY that will get your heart racing and leave you breathless by the end... (New Adult)

**The Wicked Awakened** – a Halloween novel, a five hundred year old witch wants to turn SARAH MATTHEWS' body into her new home... A twisted tale involving a coven hell bent on seeing that she succeeds. Who will come out on top in this epic battle of wills? (Mature read, 18+ for sexual content and violence)